W0254240

A Handbook for My Lover

A Handbook for My Lover

ROSALYN D'MELLO

HarperCollins *Publishers* India

First published in hardback in India in 2015 by
HarperCollins *Publishers* India

P-ISBN: 978-93-5177-640-6
E-ISBN: 978-93-5177-641-3

2 4 6 8 10 9 7 5 3 1

HarperCollins *Publishers*
A-75, Sector 57, Noida, Uttar Pradesh 201301, India
1 London Bridge Street, London, SE1 9GF, United Kingdom
Hazelton Lanes, 55 Avenue Road, Suite 2900, Toronto, Ontario M5R 3L2
and 1995 Markham Road, Scarborough, Ontario M1B 5M8, Canada
25 Ryde Road, Pymble, Sydney, NSW 2073, Australia
195 Broadway, New York, NY 10007, USA

Typeset in 11/14 Adobe Jenson Pro by
R. Ajith Kumar

Printed and bound at
Thomson Press (India) Ltd.

This is not entirely a work of fiction.

Any resemblance to characters, real or imaginary, is purely intentional.

No men were harmed in the making of this handbook.

The Dedication

dédicace / dedication

An episode of language which accompanies any amorous gift whether real or projected; and, more generally, every gesture, whether actual or interior, by which the subject dedicates something to the loved being.

—*Roland Barthes,* A Lover's Discourse

*For P.B., who doesn't 'give a fuck'**

* Then again, if you're reading this, you probably do.

CONTENTS

CONTENTS

PROLOGUE

To strip you must first wear your sins like clothes.

This act of dressing demands a scholarly acquaintance with guilt and nakedness, and an obsession with redemption. Eve, too, was initiated into the kingdom of strip when she first ate the forbidden fruit and experienced an aftertaste of shame. Adam participated, and for the first time understood what it meant to dress and undress. 'And their eyes were open,' the book of Genesis tells us. 'And they were conscious that they had no clothing and they made themselves coats of leaves stitched together.'

From them we inherited the act of stripping.

To strip you must contend with shame. You must learn to make too much of dust.

Take your time with revelation. Too much, too soon, and the epiphany of naked flesh will be irrevocably lost.

Stripping is a function of movement. Do not unravel in chronological order. Do not be distracted by time. Do not worry about sequence.

There is no law that dictates what to undo first. To start with the top-most button and make your way down to the last indicates a grievous lack of imagination.

To strip is to confess. To lay bare. To expose yourself to a pair of possibly unforgiving eyes. There is no beginning and no obvious end. Beneath the veneer of clothes is not just the naked body but a universe of skin and scars, and the memory of touch.

To strip you need an audience. A single voyeur will do.

Come in. Sit down. Keep your hands firmly on either side of your chair. Sure, you may smoke a cigarette. Even pour yourself a glass of single malt, if you like.

There's something I'd like to show you. Something that I'd like you to see. I know you've witnessed it all before, but this time it's different. This time I am going to strip while you watch. As I undo each layer, I'll make my little confessions about things I ought to have told you, things you ought to have known. We cannot proceed with the contents of this handbook until we've stepped across this line.

I've never done this before, but I've been practising. There are new things I've learned to do with my fingers, new tricks I've learned to do with my waist, new movements I've learned to make with my body. But I've yet to learn how to titillate.

I shall strip to my almost core.

Except, I'll keep that diamond on my nipple and that ruby on my cunt.

You shouldn't see too much.

({})

I first undo the straps of my sandals. My feet make contact with marble.

A few months ago, after several glasses of Laphroaig and the feast I made that we consumed, you returned to your study to work. I stacked the used plates in the sink, turned on some jazz, then proceeded to wash the dishes. It's become a habit, cleaning your kitchen after we're both done eating.

I was ravenously happy. I'd cooked Goan sausages with strips of onion and potatoes, and a hint of tamarind juice, and had stir fried beans on the side with crushed pepper, burnt garlic, and a slice of salt. You'd licked your fingers in delight. You were ravenously happy too, and right before you walked into your study, had even thanked me for having sated your appetite. As I soaped and scrubbed each plate, I sang along to Nina Simone singing '*Just in time*'. I was inebriated. By you. By vinegar. By single malt.

Sometime between Nina mouthing, '*I was lost*' and '*The losing dice were tossed*', a quarter plate slipped from my fingers and gravitated towards the floor. It took a while to register. By the time I did, the single unit that was the quarter plate had split into five.

It was irrevocable.

Your kitchen felt like a crime scene. I bent over and picked up every scrap of evidence and I scanned the floor for fingerprints that would trace the incident back to me. Then I washed my hands with soap, pulled out the comics page from the newspaper and used it to wrap the broken bits. I placed this little package in my bag, then searched for the scrubber that had fallen too. I continued with the dishwashing while battling with syntax.

I didn't break the plate.

The plate *broke itself*.

I was an innocent bystander.

For days I was saddled with guilt. I knew how attached you

were to your kitchen things, most of which were older than I was. I stashed the dismembered corpse of the broken plate in a drawer in my house, hoping it might collect itself and reincarnate. As a spoon, or a tea strainer, or a butter knife ... as anything that could be returned to you.

Weeks later the guilt dissipated, leaving behind a vindictive smirk. I felt strangely satisfied with myself. The plate was no ordinary casualty, it was the victim of my revenge for all those times you manhandled my heart, all the times you almost broke me. I carefully disguised its absence by serving breakfast in dinner plates instead. I was surprised you didn't notice. One day you might and I may not be around to plead guilty to this crime.

Yes. *I* broke your plate.

({})

I take off my earrings. My body is now unadorned.

When I was a young girl, my parents made too much of broken things. I learned to fear the sounds of breaking—waves cracking against each other and falling apart over the shore; post-pubescent boys and the hoarseness of their voices; wind galloping against trees, swishing and swooshing as somewhere in the distance clouds tumbled against clouds and rumbled with an unceasing, cacophonous laughter; sheets of glass that contained within each atom the sureness of shattering.

My mother, too, was afraid of broken things and would lock the cutlery in the kitchen cupboard, to be exhibited on special occasions. We ate in melamine plates and drank in cheap glasses. Any unintentional transgression with anything fragile was met with severe punishment: lashes of my father's belt or the snare of my mother's tongue.

I learned to hide my sins, bury them under the mattress, stash them in the backyard of my cupboard, sweep them outside the house. I learned to disassociate myself from fragments formed by lapses. Over time the secrets piled up. The crimes didn't go unnoticed but I learned to deny any involvement.

I learned, most of all, that nothing, not even the toughest fortress that surrounds the most indestructible heart, is unbreakable.

({})

My fingers slither across my back in search of hooks only to realize there's no bra to undo. So they loiter around the front and unhook my blouse. I cover my breasts with the bordered edge of my sari. The palm of my right hand encases my left breast. I can feel my pulse.

I was eleven years old the first time I got my heart broken. I've learned nothing from that experience.

I continue to expose it to too much sunlight and let it roam naked at night.

There is some small memory of agony preserved in some dark corner of my skull. I need torchlight to arrive at it. You could say I was possibly too young to know, too young to remember. I was, however, young enough to know what it felt like to hand my heart on a platter to someone who claimed to want it, and then have it returned to me, used and half-discarded, faded and dog-eared.

Never again, I decided. Except, a year later, he borrowed it again. This time I had it bubble-wrapped and insulated from within. Sometime between my giving and his discarding of my offering, I sought refuge in words. I learned to listen with my eyes and speak with my fingers. I learned to surrender uncompromisingly to the moment, to let the words dictate my actions. No harm could come to me as long as I had my tongue, as long as words raged through my blood, as long as I had the venom of language at my disposal.

I got my heart broken when I was eleven years old. I cried in secret, wrote poems in hiding, and stashed the broken pieces in a diary I've long since burned.

({})

I unravel my hair and take a few steps towards you so that I'm now at arm's length. I look at you self-consciously, as if you were a mirror.

On the wall beside my bed hangs a black-and-white photograph of you. It's a cutout from a magazine. It isn't larger than the size of my palm and yet you seem to leap out of the invisible frame.

This is the image I often wake up to: you seated casually on a cane chair, your hands wielding a digital camera as if brandishing a weapon. Your eyes intense, your gaze focused, the lens level with your forehead, the stub of a cigarette dangling between the first three fingers of your left hand.

I've placed you at a vantage point. From where I lie immersed in dreams, it would seem as though you're looking down at me, framing me, watching my every move as the morning light stretches across my skin to illuminate my contours.

I wish you'd look at me as purposefully, seek me out with your lens, frame me within the confines of your vision and leave me fixed in your gaze.

I want you to covet me with a single look. I want you to possess me with the purity of your appetite.

I want this image I have of you taped to my wall to become flesh. I want you to watch over my body being intoxicated by dreams. I want you to ache to be inside it, to be one with your subject.

({})

My fingers trail across your body until they confront your fingers. You follow every slight movement and confront the contrast between our shades. Your complexion a delicate strain of brown inherited through a combination of ancestral influences. Mine only slightly lighter than coal.

When I was twelve and self-conscious, I had a nightly ritual. I'd stand in front of the mirror, comb my hair, brush my teeth, wash my face, dry myself, then stare at my reflection, wondering if this was really me. Before sleeping I'd say a little prayer. Always, the same words coursed through my lips because there was only one thing I wanted most of all.

Beauty.

I prayed for beauty.

When I woke, I'd walk to the mirror and face my disappointment. Nothing had changed. My skin was still as dark as roasted cocoa. I'd lament the day; the jibes from strangers reminding me of my unfortunate colour, my mother's protest at my opposition to fairness creams, my dwindling self-esteem, my battle with choosing clothes whose colour wouldn't contrast so sharply against the black of my skin.

I was the misfit by default. I hated being different. I was tired of derision. I wanted to be desired.

This petitioning and the ensuing disappointment continued for two years. Until one night, when I decided to alter the texture of my intercession.

I stopped asking for beauty. I asked for wisdom instead.

It has made all the difference.

({})

My pallu slips off my shoulder and touches the floor. My breasts are exposed. I reflect light.

You've never quite acknowledged my beauty. Save for that one night, in the midst of that conversation we had about H, your temporary rival, when I explained his desire for me.

'I'm not surprised,' you said. 'You're young, and beautiful.'

'Oh! So finally you admit I'm beautiful?'

'It depends on how one defines beauty.'

'And what is your conception of beauty?'

'I think of beauty as light. Light that shines through from within ... Yes, I think you're beautiful.'

({})

I lift the edge of the pallu from the ground and tuck it between your thumb and your tallest finger. I move away from you so that the yards stretch and the sari undrapes itself. At the end of my delicate twirl I'm standing before you in nothing but my petticoat. Almost there. Almost. You look at me and smile. You gesture at me with your eyes, invite me to come closer, to inhabit the space between your legs. You draw the string that holds up my petticoat. It unfurls like a loose rose petal, and sits against your thighs. I'm naked. You explore my texture with your fingers; you linger over the birthmark below my left breast, the scar on my thigh which bears the memory of hot tea, the stretch marks that grace the inner region of my thighs, the blunt edges of the hair that veils my cunt. I place my arms against your shoulders. I lower my body so my tongue is level with your tongue. I wrap my lips around your mouth and administer a soft, delicate kiss designed to leave you wanting. I draw back and stand upright. I'm about to strut away from you when your fingers make contact with my clit. You strip me with one finger. I come undone.

How do I arrive at my truth? How many layers must I undo until you can finally touch my core? Where must I begin?

Perhaps the truth lies scattered across these pages, coded between words. You must discover it for yourself. Because, interspersed with my truth is your truth.

This striptease isn't complete until I strip you too.

If only you'd left me your keys ...

... we wouldn't be in this mess. Dust-lined floors, walls featuring dense networks of cobwebs resembling migrant settlements, withered bedcovers, frayed carpets, balconies colonized by pigeons and their prolific droppings. And rats. Four of them scurrying around playing hide-and-seek.

I wish I were exaggerating.

In your defence, not all of this is the consequence of your recent three-month long absence. The ceiling in the front bathroom and the store room has been in a state of near collapse ever since my first visit three years ago, and the decades-old paint has always been peeling off bit by silent bit. With every subsequent visit new splotches of cement have been exposed.

Ever since I can remember, your house has worn an air of ruin.

Though I'm glad to see you, I do not feel any sympathy. In fact, my body is still reeling from yesterday's chores. I'd stopped by to check on your car. The cover had blown off and was cocooned in muck. It couldn't be salvaged. The staircase leading to your house was caked in an inch-thick layer of dust, and a dog had left you a present right outside your door.

I bought a broom, borrowed a dustpan from your neighbour

and swept each filthy stair. When I was done, I asked for a bucket of water, which I took downstairs so I could wash your car that had been showered with leaves and flowers and dust and bore footprints of the rain that had sputtered all over the hood. Then I walked to the market and bought you a carton full of groceries that weighed at least five kilos. The market was half a kilometre away and my back bore the brunt of the weight.

I didn't mind. I was too ecstatic about your return. I'd fantasized about it for weeks. I'd be leaning against the glass walls of the arrivals lounge, peering through to catch a glimpse of you before you made your exit, before you could spot me. I'd be wearing a cleavage-revealing white dress; my hair would be left loose. My eyes would be lit up with joy. Finally, you'd see me and move your trolley towards me and pause. I'd fling my arms around your neck and draw you closer and not let go for a few standstill minutes. I imagined it vividly as a shot from a Kar Wai film—the rest of the world in restless motion as the two of us stood still.

Turned out you spotted me first while I was still unaware of you. I continued to peer through the glass door until I sensed your presence and turned to find you walking towards me. I hugged you with the abandon of an orphaned child. You held me for just a few seconds and let me kiss you on your cheek the way you are wont to do in the company of strangers, and then you drew away. 'Let's go home,' you said. As you walked ahead, you lit a cigarette and revelled in your overdue nicotine high.

I knew we'd be walking into a mess. I'd anticipated it and had carried a pair of shabby clothes so I could get down to housework. But I hadn't imagined the extent of the ruin. We left the luggage by the entrance and surveyed the catastrophe. Scattered grain, bits of broken glass on the kitchen floor, and a trail of footprints bore testimony to the presence of rats. I unlocked the door to the balcony and at least ten pigeons were petrified into flight. The vessels I'd washed three months ago were coated with dust. The fridge, though empty, suffered from stale breath.

I couldn't believe you'd rather abandon your house to the elements than surrender it to my care.

One hour later, I'm standing in the midst of your mess, at my wit's end, broom in one hand, dustpan in the other, surgical mask over my nose and mouth, trying hard not to curse you, trying hard to revive my excitement over your return that's fading with every newly discovered scene of destruction. I find myself muttering under my breath. This wasn't what I had in mind when we met.

How and when did your mess become my mess?

I wish I had never met you. You've been nothing but an inconvenience.

You were supposed to be a one-night stand. A quick fix. A conquest. A ten-line poem in my grand anthology of lovers.

But you seduced me. First, with your persistence, and later, after I'd relented, with your measured indifference.

I tried to resist you. I attempted an escape the first time I found myself consumed by the weight of gravity. By then you'd already interfered with the rhythm of my heartbeat so that my blood began to thin and my arteries had to work overtime to contain the flood. I confronted you about my strange condition. You said, with the air of a professional, that I was exhibiting an early symptom of that peculiar disease called love. I was confused. Last I checked I'd bulletproofed and bubble-wrapped my heart so that I'd be immune from such infections. I told you flatly that this had to end.

'You mean you're scared and you'd rather run away?' you jeered.

I held you personally responsible for my fall from grace.

You conned me. You were calculating, like a criminal. Stealthily you made inroads into my routine so that steadily, the day was no longer complete until you'd appeared in my thoughts. Before I knew it, you'd made yourself indispensable.

You were an aberration to the narrative of men I'd known. You were older. Grouchier. Celebrated. Indifferent to my beauty or lack thereof. Self-assured to a fault and yet unexpectedly vulnerable. A man with impeccable taste. So unabashedly and unapologetically yourself.

You were nothing but a disruption to my state of being. You awakened in me something more dangerous than hunger, more desperate than fervour, more potent than hatred.

This fit of madness is still at its height. Ovid was right when he was dispensing advice in his handbook, *The Cure for Love*: 'It is difficult to stop it mid-career.' I've tried. Religiously I wait for the day when it will all be undone. When the spell is lifted and I'm no longer consumed by you and you're no longer obsessed with me and we can both return to the way we were before we met—unentangled, uninhibited by love, committed to no one but ourselves.

There are no other likely endings. This affair of ours refuses to surrender to the trappings of marriage or even the non-committal everydayness of a live-in. You'd drive me up the wall with your apprehensions about space since you can't seem to trust yourself to leave me your house key.

This was doomed from the beginning.

I transgressed all norms when I chose to associate myself with you. I've been punished for my deviance. I've no choice but to put up with this exile between your home and mine, forced to live between boundaries, forced to relinquish every possibility of permanence. Your house can at best be a makeshift home for me. In your absence, when you travel the world with your cameras documenting lives in transition, I live in my rented apartment where I learn to temper my longing for you and my absurd nostalgia for a home and a life we can never share.

Like lovers without a destination, we seem fated to seek refuge in the transient.

We tried to address this once, when H seemed to want me.

'Consider it,' you said. 'I'm always away. At least he's around.'

I thought about it, but my spirit wasn't willing, neither was my flesh. I wrote to you categorically: 'Just because you're always away doesn't mean you don't deserve to have someone to come home to,' I said, digging my own grave, innocently etching my obituary into unforgetting stone—'Someone he could come home to', it would read.

I didn't fathom the extent of the mess I'd inherit through that declaration.

And yet, even in retrospect, I can see how it was inevitable.

({})

I've made my peace with the broom. Each room, I've figured, ought to be swept at least twice before I proceed to swab the floors. We've negotiated a strategy; you'd vacuum the cobwebs while I took care of the surfaces. You'd clean the toilets and the bathtub while I contended with the pigeon poo. All the vessels would have to be washed and baptised in potassium permanganate to vanquish any trace of rat prints. We agreed I'd do the dishes if you'd tackle the bedspreads and the clothes.

As I waged war with dust, I wondered if you were exploiting my youth. If you were taking advantage of my supple muscles and my capacity to care. But then I wondered if I was exploiting you, mining you for material without allowing you the privilege of being a muse.

I rant about your house when in fact I'm in love with every square-foot of it, not because it houses you but because it is such an undeniable extension of you. I love your kingdom of ruins, the looming towers of newspapers stacked upon newspapers, the bottles of single malt, green and gleaming and empty, more than there ought to be for a man with a fatty liver. Six ashtrays—two makeshift, the ruins of old music blaring from your centuries-old speakers, the fossils buried under cartons of photographs, the pen stands filled with pens with rusty nibs and dried up ink, the razor-edges of blunt scissors, the squirrel's nest by the bathroom window, so fluffy I have to resist the urge to touch it, the stains on your marble floors that have been around for years, the kitchen lined with memories of past loves, past loneliness, your cupboard a collection of clothes you refuse to surrender.

You're a hoarder in denial.

To the world you're unattached, but within these walls is all that is precious, all the ghosts from the past you can't seem to exorcise. And yet, try as I may, I cannot find traces of other women. No abandoned bangles, no hair clip, no loose strands of hair save mine, no bindi stuck against the frame of the mirror.

If an archaeologist were to survey these ruins, he'd have to bring in a collegium of scholars and carbon-dating machines. I wonder if they'd find what I've found, remnants of your heart beating wildly with a rhythm that hasn't yet lost its pace, despite your cynicism, despite your bitterness. A smouldering bit of bloody flesh that refuses to rot, refuses to ash, a thing of terrible beauty, immense and glorious, full of depth and soul. Unbroken still.

Unlike mine.

Perhaps it is love that dictates my dedication. I've never quite admitted to being in love with you, neither have you. We've left it as something yet to be understood and acknowledged. We haven't yet made an ideal of it. We haven't yet made a mess of it. The only evidence we have is encrypted in the language of gestures.

As my body melts into sweat, as sweat mingles with dust, as heat and dust collide, as the floor reveals itself with each stroke of broom and cloth, I'm convinced that love isn't many-splendoured or virtuous. It is a dirty, beleaguered thing. I wonder if Jimmy Porter, the angry young man in John Osborne's play *Look Back in Anger*, was right when he told his wife Alison, 'It's no good fooling about with love, you know. You can't fall into it like a soft job without dirtying your hands. It takes muscle and guts. If you can't bear the thought of messing up your nice, tidy soul, you better give up the whole idea of life and become a saint, because you'll never make it as a human being.'

({})

Day two.

It was evening all afternoon. It was raining and it was about to rain. My back had given way after all the sprucing. I took a pill and fell asleep on the bed while you worked in your study. I woke up and made a pot of Castleton.

'What else can I do?' I asked.

'If you could just wave a magic wand and make all of this go away? Like in the movies, just a single swoosh and everything that was messy is suddenly in order,' you said.

'You're confusing me with Mary Poppins,' I said and smiled and meant it.

Three hours later, when we reconvened on the marble-top table-for-two for some single malt, you were amazed by the transformation.

'I see you waved your magic wand.' you said. 'Are you working?' you asked.

'Yes, I was writing about the rats.'

'Why?'

'Because you told me to.'

Last evening two rats had walked into your trap. You'd called me to see for myself. I was afraid if I made conversation with them, I might feel the urge to adopt them.

'Come on, say hello,' you said. 'Maybe you can write about them.'

'Is that a challenge?'

'Maybe.'

I watched the two rats. One of them was resigned to his captivity. Maybe that one was your embodiment. He sat idly in a corner and awaited his fate while his companion who, I imagined was my animal counterpart, seemed determined to push herself through the narrow bars and escape.

Later, when we went to release the couple in the wilderness

behind your house, I wasn't surprised when one rat made a quick getaway and pranced out of the cage while the other had to be cajoled into leaving.

'Come on,' you urged him.

'Stockholm syndrome,' I said.

I thought of Barthes' definition of Catastrophe: Violent crisis during which the subject, experiencing the amorous situation as a definitive impasse, a trap from which he can never escape, sees himself doomed to total destruction.

As we sipped the peaty Ardbeg you'd bought, duty-free, I wanted to ask you if you felt the same way about the rats; if, like me, you saw in them a reflection of our catastrophe. But you distracted me.

'So, if I'd told you *not* to write about the rats, would you *not* have written about them?'

'No. You can't control what I don't write just as I can't control what I write.'

'Do I figure prominently in what you're writing?' you asked.

'Maybe.'

'So when you're done, should I go through it with red ink and cross off the parts that misrepresent me?'

'You could, but it wouldn't deter me. Don't worry; I haven't revealed your identity. I haven't used your name. Just your initials, and only once, in the dedication.'

({})

I have my doubts about whether you'll even read this from start to finish. I debated writing it to begin with, especially since you're such a reluctant reader. But I took Barthes' advice. *To know that one does not write for the other, to know that these things I am going to write will never cause me to be loved by the one I love, to know that writing compensates for nothing, sublimates nothing, that it is precisely there where you are not—this is the beginning of writing.*

It's a peculiar book I'm writing. It isn't a love letter. It isn't an ode. It pretends to be an instruction manual, but only succeeds in parts. I prefer to call it a handbook, or a survival kit, or an *episode of language*. I know I said it was, but it isn't quite dedicated to you. Rather, it is directed at you.

It was something I started a year ago, after a conversation with you over the phone after midnight, a few months after we first began, long-distance. I was in Bombay, the city of my childhood. You were home in Delhi. I heard my phone ring just as I was about to sleep. It was the ringtone I'd reserved for your calls, Madeleine Peyroux's version of Cohen's '*Dance me to the end of love*'. We exchanged details about the day. Mine was charmed as usual. I'd spent hours staring into the sea, as if in search of some epiphany. Your body burned in Delhi's afternoon heat and the sky sent no breezes to quell you at twilight.

I can't recall exactly how it came to pass, but the conversation drifted to an old flame of mine (he who could make the violins come). Yes, I had spotted him that morning and he had appeared luminous, as if he had swallowed all of last night's stars and his skin had begun to gleam. You were confused. Justifiably. Who was this ex-flame? What was his co-ordinate on my map of lost lovers? Did he come before or after you? Did he like my taste? Was he still attuned to my scent? Had I mentioned him before or had I just constructed him out of thin air?

'How many lovers have you had?' you asked, your voice carefully disguising each word so that the question mark at the end of your statement would seem like genuine curiosity. Except, it wasn't really a question. There was a tinge of sarcasm and an unmistakable hint of jealousy.

'You're one to talk!'

'Well, I'm much older than you. It's only natural that I've had a few.'

'Maybe someday I'll tell you. When you've earned the right to know.'

({})

If you are indeed reading this, it's too late. You've wandered into my trap. You chose to sink your teeth into the apple's hard flesh. Now you must eat of it until you arrive at its core, until its bitter seeds unravel upon your tongue.

We began with the body.
You and I.

Our first 'date'. I am ushered into the living room of your absent friend's home in Bombay. I peep through a door on the right and find you tinkering with your laptop. On the dining table stands a half-empty glass of wine. I announce my presence. You emerge from the bedroom. We shake hands.

We've never met before, except on Facebook chat.

You pour me a glass of red wine; my poison. I slump into the sofa across from you. Before I can even begin to sip my wine, you start to investigate, decipher. You want to break me down into chewable fragments so you can piece together the story of my short-lived life. I indulge you. Rarely have I been the subject of such curiosity.

We evade the body.

I stick to your eyes, steer clear of your lips. You prefer to look away. Your gaze is focused on tangible things like the glass in your hand, the wild red roses that stick out of the short vase in which they were stashed, the bookshelves filled with titles neither of us would ever read.

We talk until we reach a pause. A gap. I'm unsure what to say next. So are you. So you leave me alone in the front room and walk into the bedroom. When you step back out, J.J. Cale is singing the blues:

A perfect woman, she's got no rules
Soft to the touch, silky smooth
She got everything a man could use
Ain't no doubt about it, when we make love
She's good down under, she's good up above

Nice move.

Three glasses down. My head is swirling in a crimson haze. I need to stay still so I focus on you; the soft twirls of your hair, the black and white tufts of your beard, the way your body sways to the beat and your fingers keep time on the hard brown wood of the table that supports your feet. You sift through a blue pouch, slip out a film of paper upon which you stack a small heap of tobacco. With sleight of hand and flick of tongue you roll yourself a cigarette. You roll another for me. I don't smoke but I want my mouth to taste like yours.

I watch and learn. I observe how you hold the butt between your fingers, how your fingers move so deftly between air and lip so that now the cigarette is alight. You take a drag. Your breath wets the paper.

Presumptuously, you pour me another glass. You draw the rim toward your lips, sip, smile, then tap your toes to Cale.

We delay.

We defer that moment of contact we both know we want. We're unsure of how to seize the chance to make lips graze. We dilly-dally. Meaningless chatter about theatre and poetry and photography. Words are poor substitutes for touch. All I want is a mindful fuck, an exquisite escape into the ethereal, a feast of sin and flesh, excess.

The clock is ticking. It's near midnight, the Cinderella hour. So much anguish about how to cross over to your side of the room, how to engage with the texture of your skin, so much inhibition. I cannot guess your age but you've lived at least two decades longer than I have, I imagine, and I'm hoping you'll heed to your superior wisdom and say something intelligent, something that will lead to touch. You've whetted my appetite, what I want now is an opportunity to bite through your flesh, rummage through your skin.

I can't tell if you're the hunter and I'm the prey or if it's the other way around. You're new territory for me; your body seethes, your eyes are alive, aflame.

I'm restless. I walk across the room. You follow me with your gaze. We continue with our distracting conversation. I venture into the inner room and discover the beautiful four-post bed cloistered by a beige canopy peopled with embroidered birds and leaves and fruit. I sit by the edge and dangle my legs like a coy girl child. You stand twelve inches away. Too far. Too inaccessible. You drink your wine indifferently. For a moment I wonder if I'm imposing on your time.

I'm drunk and I'm hungry and I want to make a feast of you. I want to nail you against the mattress and bite into your muscles, chew on your past. I want to carve my initials on your flesh so you won't ever forget this hazy evening and all the redundant talk about politics and art, all the meaningful moments of delay.

You draw closer. I invite you to sit beside me. We talk, softly this time. By now we've understood the worthlessness of words. Your breath sticks to me, clings to my skin. I say something silly, you turn your head towards me and bits of laughter spill over. I tilt my head so I can face you but you turn away at that very moment so my lips graze lightly against your beard. An accident. Until you realign yourself so that your mouth is now right above mine, and your tongue slips between my lips and makes small talk with my tongue.

Almost midnight.

I have to leave.

I pull away, undone. It is unfinished but I have to go.

'Pity,' you say.

'You had all night ... I was willing ...'

'One has to take the time to get to know someone,' you reply.

I want you to know me in a biblical way.

You reach for one last kiss. You pin me against the wall and in the middle of our rapturous conversation reach for the edges of my kurta which you then roll over my head and cast away. You're pleasantly surprised to discover there's no lacey bra underneath for you to unhook.

'I *have* to go,' I beseech one last time. You press yourself against my cunt as if your lust is reason enough for me to stay.

It is ...

'You're not going anywhere,' you say.

'Even if I wanted to ... I can't. I'm menstruating.'

'So what? It's completely natural,' you say after you've unbuttoned my jeans.

I unfasten your shirt, undo your trousers, kiss parts of you that only I can reach with my tongue.

You leave me for a minute, walk to the bathroom to slip on a condom. When you return, you're naked, except for the condom. You hold two sets of newspapers in your hands.

'*Times of India* or *Indian Express*,' you ask.

'*Times of India*. Thicker paper. Dispensable.'

You lay a few centre spreads across the expensive linen that lines the bed and proceed to fuck me.

You come inside me and refuse to leave. You release the weight of your body upon mine. After the final thrust, after the last blow, you gasp and then crash into sleep in my arms as my fingers trail along the warm, pulse-stricken expanse of your skin. Our hearts tap away, loud and quick, gasping with relief.

Outside, clouds begin to weep, lightning strikes, followed by the ominous clamour of thunder.

I cajole you out of your post-coital slumber. It's beyond late. I have to leave.

You waltz around the room and look for your displaced trousers, fish for your wallet and hand me a few notes.

'I hope you won't take this the wrong way, but cabs are expensive.'

I'm too broke to refuse your offer.

You wrap a crisp white towel across your waist, escort me to the elevator and bid me goodbye with a kiss.

'Can I see you again before I leave?' you ask.

'Maybe.'

We moved from body to being.

One day later.

Muggy evening. Intermittent drizzles. Our second encounter. Café Mondegar. Bombay.

Your feet graze against mine under the table. The glutinous jukebox makes music out of coins. The waiter places a six-glass pitcher of beer between us. You pour a glass each and move the pitcher aside. You spread regions of your life across the mug-ringed table. Your fingers serve as a compass, guiding me through twists and turns.

Until you reach an intersection that brings us back to the night before.

'I was surprised. I didn't expect it to lead to where it did,' you say.

'I find that hard to believe,' I reply in between sips of beer.

'Well, I'm not the young buck I used to be.'

'When was the last time you were spontaneous like that?'

'A while ago. I was in New York. She must have been a few years younger than you.'

'How old would that make her?'

'She must have been about twenty-eight, I guess.'

'I turned twenty-three three weeks ago.'

Pause.

For a while I debated whether to ask about your age. I tried to decipher from the clues I'd been given; the salt-and-pepper of your beard and your hair, the lines across your brow, but I couldn't hazard a guess. Perhaps it was better not to know.

'I'm fifty-three,' you say.

'So what happened with the girl in New York? Why didn't it work out?'

'She couldn't get over the difference in age. She let me go.'

Pause.

The waiter sets a plate of beef chilly fry on the table, followed by a plate of stuffed mushrooms.

'It's good to be in a place where not too many people know me,' you say.

(I'm flummoxed by that little piece of dialogue. I didn't know then who you were. Later I'd understand. Then I just saw you as exceedingly interesting and eminently fuckable. I didn't know of your fame. I knew you had talent. I'd seen your exhibition months ago in Delhi. Those stunning black-and-white photographs you'd taken when you were even younger than I am now. That self-portrait in a room you'd once called home, your eyes all droopy from a trippy, purple-hazed night. The cupboard behind you is unlocked, but your body is open and inviting. You're looking into the lens inside-out and outside-in. I remember looking for you in each image but you seemed elusive. Evasive. Nomadic. Wanderlusting between spaces, observing, living on the fringe between the world of the living and the realm of the bystander, peeping through a hole, as it were, with wonder and surprise, and capturing in perfect compositions the miracle of the familiar, the ordinary.)

We finish our beer. It's time to leave. We hail a cab. I should have taken one myself, and headed to my home at the other end of the city, but I step into your cab instinctively. It doesn't strike you as odd. We sit in silence, smothered by the monsoon breeze. You light a cigarette. I reach for your left hand.

Sparks.

'What are you thinking?' I ask, expecting some romantic retort.

'I'm thinking about how I need to take a piss!'

We're now in your room. You take your much-awaited piss. I sit on the edge of that beautiful, four-poster bed and await your next move. You walk past me, take off your shirt and dive into bed. I'm *in media res*. I'd slipped my sandals off and was about to lie down beside you when I heard your half-order, half-plea.

'Massage.'

With that single word you tow the line between one-night stand and lover. It's more than I'm looking to provide.

Fucking is fucking, there's something definite about it; the certainty of destination. Fucking depends on the emergency of lust. A massage, on the other hand, demands a profound understanding of the body. You want more than a quick run-through of the connections between limb and torso and muscle and bone. You want more than precision. You seek the kind of touch that can brand itself permanently in some way. The sort of touch your muscles will remember.

I am not prepared for this.

I fake ignorance.

'It isn't my forte,' I lie.

'I'll instruct you.'

You direct every tiny move like a backseat driver. You tell me where to pause, where to punctuate, and how; where to stress and where to glide over; where to linger and where to stay, and for how long.

I follow each instruction. As I knead your flesh, I am inspired by it. Your back is smooth and clear, the skin soft yet taut, betraying your age. With each fresh contact I find myself growing moist. I want to focus on the pathways, which, if pressed precisely, will relax, but I'm distracted by the rush of blood coursing through your body, inflecting the undercurrents of my bloodstream.

You drift into a genre of half-baked sleep.

I take liberties with your body. Lips replace fingers. I kiss all your delicate by-lanes, your short cuts, the highway that is your spine, and the nape of your neck. I peck at your ear lobe and lick the edges with the softness I otherwise reserve for wild strawberries.

You stir. Turn over. I press my lips against your lips and return to your ear lobe. I'm crouched over your body. I can feel the stir of your flesh rising to greet me.

'I have to go. It's late. I shouldn't even be here,' I say.

'You can't get me all turned on like this and then threaten to leave.'

So I stay until I've satisfied myself. Until you've ravished me with the bulk of your lust.

'Spend the night with me,' you say.

'I wish I could. But you leave tomorrow. I'd rather we don't get attached.'

'Let me drop you half-way then.'

You do, until the Peddar Road junction. You ask the cabbie how much the fare would be and pay him in advance.

({})

Five days later.

Delhi Airport. Baggage claim. Failed attempts to quieten my brain.

Why am I here? Is there any wisdom to this trip? What sense in prolonging a goodbye, delaying it, deferring it?

You were supposed to be a one-night stand. A bookmark. A ten-line poem in my grand anthology of lovers.

But you had more sinister designs.

I had every intention of relegating you to memory. In fact, just before what should have been our final kiss in that black-and-yellow taxi in Mumbai, I'd looked you in the eyes, smiled and asked if you'd remember me after the spell had been lifted.

I cannot remember your reply. But I suppose I'm implicated too for I messaged you the next day, on an impulse, saying, 'I remember you already.'

You responded with a phone call.

'Come to Delhi!' you said.

'I will, when I find the time. I have other loose ends I need to tie up there in any case.'

'So why not come now?'

'I'm not exactly good on funds at the moment. First job. First month. Still to receive my first cheque.'

Pause.

'Won't you be back in Bombay for a day or two in another two weeks? Some opening or the other?' I say.

'Yes, but that'll be too touch and go. We won't have the luxury of time.'

Pause.

'What if I subsidize your fare?' you petition.

'I wouldn't be comfortable with that. Once bitten twice shy, like they say.'

'What do you mean?'

'Well, my ex once paid for a ticket for me to visit him, and after we broke up, he wanted his money back.'

'I wouldn't do such a thing.'

'That's what they all say.'

'Maybe you can do something in exchange. Maybe you can write about my work.'

'Go on.'

'You said you like it, maybe you can write to me and tell me why.'

'That seems doable.'

'How soon can you get here?'

'This weekend? I can leave the office early on Friday and take a flight.'

'Let me speak to my agent.'

Your next message contained a PNR.

Absurd. Flying out to see someone I'd only fucked twice.

'Do you remember anything about our first night?' I asked in reply to your email.

'It's all a blur. Maybe that's why I'm asking you to come.'

Delhi Airport. Baggage in hand, I stand along the edge of the road, waiting for you to pick me up. I feel like one of Bukowski's women. Fortunately, you're much better looking and not half as alcoholic.

You swing by in your Gypsy. You're dressed in a dark blue cotton shirt. You look gorgeous, the salt and pepper of your beard contrasts against the deep hue. I dump my bag in the backseat and get in. You hit the accelerator and we're in motion. It's an old car. You've had it forever, I can tell. It makes a grumpy sound now and then, but is steady nonetheless. I cannot imagine you in any other kind of car. I notice for the first time this habit you have of occasionally stroking your beard when you're driving.

'Welcome to Delhi,' you say when we reach the first red light and you follow it with a quick kiss. My body blushes.

I remember why I came.

({})

A year later.

Foggy evening. My third visit. Single malt.

The details escape me. I was inebriated. But at some point you tell me about your relationships with other women, your travel companions with whom you shared a bed without feeling the urge to indulge. It suddenly strikes me that I'm a complete aberration to your narrative of lovers past.

'Why was it different with me? You slept with me the first night we met,' I reminded you.

'I was very attracted to you. Maybe I shouldn't have,' you said.

'You mean you regret it?'

'I didn't say I regret it. Just that it was probably not the right thing to do.'

({})

You were supposed to be a one-night stand, a bookmark, a ten-line poem in my grand anthology of lovers.

But you refused to play the part. You weren't interested

in temporary delights. You took charge and steered us into unchartered waters. Despite the distance between us, despite our separate lives, despite our individual penchant for solitude, we stumbled into this black hole, this point of no return, this movement from lust to love, from body to being.

I moved.

For selfish reasons.

One: I found I was allergic to distances. My body began to break out periodically into bouts of longing, my blood began to thicken with the constant weight of your absence, my heart started to suffer for lack of permanence, and my fingers grew weary for want of your pulse throbbing over its tips.

Two: In the course of my research it became imperative that I be closer to you, my muse. So I found myself a source of employment and moved from my city-by-the-sea to your city-of-djinns.

You must have been petrified. For weeks you were in denial; you weren't convinced I'd actually go through with it. When you gathered I was intent on moving, you tried to dissuade me. You said I ought to focus on finishing my book instead of wasting time meeting with brokers, negotiating the rent, building a new life. 'Man does not live on words alone,' I tried to explain. Besides, I was steadily going broke. You then offered to support me financially on the condition that I would stay put and finish what I'd started. I couldn't decide whether you were being instinctively generous or plain cowardly.

So I took a risk and moved; collected all my things, my

books, my clothes, scraps of cash that I'd earned from here and there and comprised my meagre bank account, and set up base in a one-room barsati overlooking the Hauz Khas tombs. A few weeks into my move, you sought revenge, you started to harass me about the book. You'd wield your tongue like a whip and castigate me for my lack of pace and discipline, my bohemian lifestyle and my wayward friends, none of which, you decided, were a good influence.

I began to negotiate with you for more time. 'It's only just getting interesting,' I told you. In truth, I was repelled by the initial draft of my first chapter. It was induced by the most belligerent bout of longing I'd ever experienced, around the beginning of our second year together, when you'd spent at least six months away in Paris, photographing Indian émigrés. Every now and then, a few lines from that draft return to haunt me, and I cringe when I think about the pathos of lines like 'These pages make love to you. If you were here I'd tease you with my tongue. I'd mouth your name and listen as each syllable turns to song, and I'd roll each note along the edge of your ear … You live in the ground floor of all my songs.' Too desperate for my own good.

It wasn't something I could change overnight. The problem was not so much the quality of the lines but the attitude they reflected. I came across as a female Cyrano, doomed to unrequited love, which wasn't the case. What was required was a shift in the way I processed your absence. The original blueprint demanded that I submit myself unabashedly to the intensity of my passion for you while also salvaging my dignity. It demanded a confession that I was unwilling to make. It's so much easier to add a missable 'love you' at the end of a phone conversation. I was not prepared to make such a declaration face-to-face, or even within the expanse of these pages.

The book demanded a massive leap of faith, a crossing over that went beyond mere movement from my city to yours. It entailed that I come to terms with our fate, and trust, nonetheless, in the merit of the ephemeral—just because we knew we had no shot at a future didn't mean we weren't entitled to a present and a past.

Moreover, we hadn't fathomed the extent of our involvement. Until I moved I was just a voice over the phone you'd grown accustomed to, and a body you would reacquaint yourself with on occasion.

You weren't prepared for the ordinariness of everyday love.

Neither was I.

Two years later I could say for certain that the move was the best twist I could have ever conceived for this book. I've found, in the course of my research, that you have disabused me of every notion I ever had of a permanent home. I've realized that all I did when I adopted your city was exchange one form of exile for another.

At any given moment, I roam the city with two bags. The smaller one has my phone, my wallet, my cigarettes, my moleskines and some loose change. The bigger knapsack has my laptop and charger, my hard disk, my phone charger, three different books, a change of clothes, a pouch with tiny bottles of shampoo, conditioner and moisturizer; a kajol pencil and sharpener, lingerie, and accessories. It's my overnight bag that I carry at all times because I never know for certain when you'll ask me to come over and spend the night.

In the beginning we had a plan. We'd decide well in advance when I was to come over. There was a comfortable rhythm to our evenings together. I'd return to you after a long day of work, we'd share a glass or two of single malt over a dinner I cooked, and we'd eventually mediate the territory of your bedroom.

Over weeks, the frequency of our meetings increased. We'd find excuses to spend the night together. I'd abandon all prior engagements and run to you, vegetables in tow, and we'd revel in each other's company. By now you'd made peace with my move. You had enough exposure to the convenience of having me around to recognize it was a good thing.

Until work intervened and demanded you travel, often for between two weeks to a month. I began to lead two lives; one when you were out of town, and one when you returned.

When you were away, I'd work hard on disengaging from you. I'd hack away at the roots that entwined us. I'd attempt an escape. I'd sample other men, other tongues, other lives, and I'd convince myself that I was cured, that I had finally outgrown my lust for you, that I could indeed survive, hell, thrive in your absence. The tone of my writing changed for the better. It finally had that tinge of self-respect that it lacked before.

Then you'd return and I'd regress into love again. We'd revive our little rituals and, as your skin renewed contact with mine, we'd renew our lust.

You held all the cards. You made all the rules. I could only meet you if I was willing to schedule you as priority, which meant I had to place on hold the life I'd invented for myself in your absence and, once again, ensure that my plans revolved around you. I had to show up at your door latest by eight, else you'd claim 'it didn't make sense'. I had to choose between you and the ten million other things that the city regularly hosts. At some point my early morning work schedule got to you, so you decided we should reserve our meetings for the weekend instead. We tried it for a few weeks until we lapsed and everything went haywire all over again. A few months later, I quit my job. It seemed to come in the way of my novelistic pursuit.

If only you could leave me your keys!

A year passed. By now, we'd evolved our own systems. By now, I'd colonized your kitchen. By now, you'd already tricked me into believing I shared your house when, in fact, I was and remain a frequently visiting guest. Your only houseguest.

There were two options at hand.

One: you could leave me your keys so I could visit when I wanted and park myself in your house at will.

Two: you could make room for me in your already crowded house, nothing flamboyant, just a shelf or two to keep my things.

We veered towards option two, but too many episodes got in the way. I couldn't deal with your sudden tantrums, when, for no concrete reason you'd tell me to 'Get out'. So I'd leave, despite the lateness of the hour, and then I'd find myself returning because I had grown roots in your house. I had too many things all over the place, and they kept bringing me back.

So I decided I wouldn't leave my belongings with you, despite the many times you pleaded that I should. I had to preserve my dignity. I needed to have the option of leaving you at any given hour without having to worry about the 'Chinese cigarette case'[1].

---

[1]'*Grounds for divorce*' (2008), Elbow (*There's a Chinese cigarette case, and the rest you can keep, and the rest you can keep*)

But I slowly became part of your neighbourhood, part of the ecosystem of your house. You had to rely on me for grocery lists, for lost items, for details of leftovers. You came to depend on my spare pair of eyes to read the expiry dates on Gelusil bottles and Crocin strips, and on my spare pair of hands to scratch the itch on your back or smoothen the bundle of nerves along your right thigh when your sciatica acted up.

Which brings us to the second twist in this narrative for which there is no easy resolution: how do we confront the fact of our interdependent yet independent lives? How do we undo this mess we've found ourselves in?

And here you are asking me to quicken the pace of this treatise, begging me to seek answers to questions I'm still unable to frame, coaxing me to reveal to you everything I promised I would, while you're still unwilling to entrust me with your keys; those few hundred grams worth of metal that hold the secret to the future perfect.

Here's my last offer—a book for a key. Take it or leave it. But decide now, before we proceed, for the next section is the beginning of the end. If you choose to read further, you hereby surrender all rights to a life of solitude. If you sign against the dotted line, you must make available an extra set of keys, failing which you will have made a mockery of this handbook.

Mine is a conditional love.

What I See in You

One night, after a petty, meaningless fight, you walked into bed as if it were the sea. I dived in too, but instead of keeping to the other side of the shore as I am prone to do in the aftermath of a hurricane, I swam over and lay beside you. You climbed onto me as if you were shipwrecked and I was the only log of wood in sight for miles.

You were fishing for forgiveness. I had already forgiven you. You had sprung a leak inside my soul. It was just like you to row me gently and then threaten to have me capsize.

'What the fuck do you see in me anyway?' I said.

'Well, I could ask you the same thing,' was your cocky reply.

You then curled your back against my belly and drew my hand over your chest like the edges of a quilt and fell asleep.

I've spent months mulling over that question. What is it that I see in you? And how different is it from who you really are or seem to be?

({})

I see an arrogant man with too many lines on his palms, as if you've lived through so many lifetimes your body is struggling to adapt and can no longer keep track. There are long lines and split lines, curved lines and faint lines, bruised lines and chipped lines, smooth lines and dark lines that intersect with your head, heart, and life lines. When I read between all the lines I look to see if I've been written onto your body, if I was ever part of the script; if I'm a co-ordinate, an intersection between latitudes and longitudes; if I'm a bright, sizzling star in your constellation or if I'm just a meteor, a passing delight. Your fingers are broad and long. When you close them to make a fist, I get a brief gist of how big your heart must be. In the beginning I accused you of having bulletproofed it so you were impervious to my affection. You assured me it was as naked and wounded as mine.

({})

I see an aggressive man who conducts himself with more style and confidence than I could ever muster. You get away with too much. You are respected for your rabid intolerance of mediocrity, revered for your irreverence, saluted for your tendency to shoot from the hip, to say things that sting and to yet be loved for your brutal honesty. You don't indulge in the art of mincing words, and you don't make small talk. You're no gentleman. You're a grouch; hot-tempered and belligerent, and yet kind and compassionate.

Plath had a point in her poem '*Daddy*':

Every woman adores a Fascist
The boot in the face, the brute
Brute heart of a brute like you.

({})

You like to prolong the life of things. You're the only man I know who still drives a Gypsy. You've had it for years, I can tell, and like your body, it's beginning to deteriorate. The lining of the seats is wearing thin, the rear-view mirror to the left of the dashboard has come off and refuses to be reattached, the engine growls when the wheels are in motion, like a restless chest-beating rebel, and the carburetor throws more tantrums than a bratty five-year-old boy. It's not like you can't afford a brand-new car. You're just so attached to this machine, and I can't blame you. It's a gorgeous beast with a masculine guile. Anyone else would have given up by now. It's exhausting to have to pull over in the throes of the afternoon heat, or amidst peak-hour traffic, just to open the hood and bang the carburetor with a spanner until it is disciplined into submission so you can be on your way.

'Can't you replace the carburetor?' I asked one day.

'I could, but I'd rather get it fixed,' you said.

'So why haven't you got it fixed?' I asked.

'Because no mechanic seems to remember how to,' you mumbled. 'That's the thing about the time we're living in. We've forgotten to repair things, we prefer to replace them instead, get new parts in exchange for the old.'

I once had a lover who was too callous with everyday things. His bed was always unmade, his room always seemed like a hurricane had thrown up on the floor. His books were always dusty, his clothes were strewn around, and his kitchen sink was always spilling over with dishes. He had a penchant for misplacing things. He was so clumsy with his fingers he once ripped a 500-rupee note accidentally while fishing it out from his wallet to pay the restaurant bill.

He was a writer too, so I forgave him his inadequacies, treated them as quirks, as eccentricities. But I always knew I could never be with him beyond the present tense. It isn't wise to give your heart to a man with butter fingers.

But you—you are graceful with your fingers. There's poetry in the way you stroke your beard while you're driving, the way you sign against your prints, the way you hold a knife, the way you adjust your lens and shoot.

You refuse to give up on things, carburetors, water heaters, air conditioners, amplifiers, crusty ceilings and sun-baked walls. As long as there is an ounce of life, or the promise of resurrection, you refuse to abandon them. You hoard them. You prefer to renew their lease on life.

({})

Anne Carson makes a surprising statement in her elusively titled book, *The Beauty of the Husband, a Fictional Essay in 29 Tangos*, her poetic treatise on her liar of a husband who was 'loyal to nothing' and who she yet loved from 'early girlhood to late middle age,' who was indecent enough to send divorce papers in the mail. In the second tango, she tells the reader quite frankly why she continued to love this brute of a man. 'Beauty,' she says. 'No great secret. Not ashamed to say I loved him for his beauty. As I would again if he came near.'

Beauty convinces. You know beauty makes sex possible.
Beauty makes sex sex.
You if anyone grasp this—

Sometimes I wonder if I would have loved you had the circumstances been different, had I been born closer to your generation, had I known you when you were still in the crux of youth. You were outright gorgeous then, eyes as intense as burning coal, you of cocky smile and sunburnt skin, your hair still flaming black without a single strand of grey. I look at your self-portraits when you were the age I am now, and I marvel at your beauty. I look at your photographs of your then lover, the one with the kohl-lined eyes, and I'm envious of her beauty. I know I could never compare. You are known for all the women you've bedded, each one uniquely compelling, I am told. I've seen the pictures you've made of them lying in unmade beds, wrapped in sheets, glowing in the unmistakable light of post-coital love.

I could have had any other man I wanted. But you fixated me, despite your now middle-aged eyes, your more-salt-than-pepper hair, your still-bristling beard, or perhaps because of it. You'd been tempered by time, the creases on your forehead had taken shape, the pudge of your belly was more defined.

Maybe it's because you still have no signs of a bald spot or a receding hairline. Or maybe I enjoy feeding off your age. I remember one day when you were unwell and I decided to play nurse. I asked if there was anything at all I could do for you, massage your feet, bring you breakfast in bed, cook you a meal. You didn't want anything of the sort.

'There must be something I can do for you?' I pleaded.

'Give me back my youth?'

You are beautiful. Each time I see you I am confronted once again by your beauty, by the utterly gorgeous twist of your lips, the suave, sexy way in which you orchestrate your body, the way you walk, the deep baritone of your voice that resounds within the walls of my body, the broad sweep of your palms and the taut feel of your calves.

Above all else, it is beauty that I see in you; a strain of beauty that I am powerless to resist.

({})

Barthes, in *A Lover's Discourse*, speaks of the condition of 'atopos', which translates as 'unclassifiable, of a ceaselessly unforeseen originality'.

The loved being is recognized by the amorous subject as 'atopos', he says. Being atopic, the other makes language indecisive; one cannot speak of the other, about the other; every attribute is false, painful, erroneous, awkward: the other is 'unqualifiable'.

I find I am struggling with words.

If you were a 'type', this whole exercise would have been much simpler. But I've never known anyone like you before, and haven't since encountered anyone similar. In fact, I could argue that is half the problem—the fact that I'm no longer drawn to other men, because there's an undefined set of attributes you possess which they presumably lack.

({})

Alain de Botton, in *The Romantic Movement*, reminds us of a quote from George Bernard Shaw: 'Love is only a curious process of exaggerating the difference between one person and another.'

Somewhere, the two questions get conflated: why I love you, and what I see in you. Both are impossible to answer because of the complicated constructions of each question. For the moment, I've chosen to deal with the second question, what I see in you, but I realize how immensely subjective my answers must be. In the beginning you accused me of being too starry-eyed about you. I insisted you misunderstood my way of seeing and I maintain that position.

I've always had a sixth sense about men. All I need is to spend three intense days with a man and I can then enlist for myself all the many quirks and kinks about him that would drive me up the wall. The butter-fingered lover, for instance, had this way of softly clicking his lips together each time he spoke. It was charming at first, more an ethnic trait than something unique to him. But it steadily began to grate on my nerves until I couldn't stand it any more. Added to this was also the fact that he, like a few others, had fallen too irrevocably in love with me. He had made a fucking myth out of me.

You haven't erred yet on that front, and there is no immediate danger that you will anytime soon. That's your edge. It will soon be four years, and I still don't have a list of things that annoy me about you. There is nothing I would like to change about you. Yes, there are some amendments I'd like to prescribe, but nothing severe, nothing that would alter you in any significant way.

This is not to say I don't see your faults. You have many. I haven't put you on a pedestal. But maybe there's a case to be made for the way in which you administer varied doses of hope and despair so that at no point can I rest assured about your feelings towards me. You keep me on my toes. You don't care for stability, certainty.

You only know the gospel of flux, of eternal change. You demand the impossible of me. You are my joy and my suffering; my jury, executioner and judge. You insist on pushing me to the edge of the cliff, even nudging me on occasion. You make me falter with my speech. I feel the ground slipping under my feet, and just as I am about to fall off the precipice, you draw out a rope and pull me into the safety net of your embrace. That's the thing—I can never trust you to rescue me, and yet you do. Unfailingly.

Charter of Demands

Perhaps when we find ourselves wanting everything, it is because we are so dangerously close to wanting nothing.

—Sylvia Plath

I will not be moderate.

I want everything from life or nothing at all.

I am disgusted by lives that go on come what may, by the promise of a humdrum happiness provided I don't ask too much of life.

I want everything!

I want everyday things: vessels of stainless steel, spoons with secrets cast upon their skin, bread from three days ago left untouched in the fridge and fruits I've plucked from orchards of ill repute.

I want my garden of earthly delights with all the seven deadly sins for company.

No, I am not meek or humble, pure in heart or selfless. And I don't want paradise with its happy endings and countless beginnings.

I want a feast of sin and flesh. I want this world, not the next.

I want this body with its cellulite and sensuality and not some untainted other. I want this weight, these lines that stretch across my skin, the rings that mark my tender age, the scars that mark my experience and all the wounds that never healed.

I want a share of everything that's mine and everything that isn't.

I want a tongue that's unrestrained, uncensored, rife with obscenities.

I want Miles on his trumpet wailing as I wail.

I want you with all your empty promises, you with your tongue of fire.

I want your house too.

I want your vessels with their receding sheen, the cane furniture you inherited from some other lifetime and your bed that's lined with all your dreams.

Give me your cotton shirts and your dirty linen and I will show you the terror of a housewife. I'll fill your kitchen with blueberry pies and make you all kinds of spicy combinations to please your seasoned appetite.

I'll accost you with the violence of everyday things: morning tea and evening single malt in crockery I've inherited from generations of hospitality.

I'll ring roses around your bed and polish your floors with my lust.

I'll inscribe my name on all your letterheads, wreak havoc on your household and punish you with my words.

I'll poison you with my body. Everywhere you tread, on cobblestone footpaths or unmade beds, my scent will be sure to follow.

I'll mark your body with bruises that will glow in the naked sunlight.

I'll haunt you with more happiness than you can bear. Nothing humdrum or predictable, everyday a surprise.

You could never complain about spiders in your study or dust among your books. Your bathroom will reek of my peach-scented lotion and every morning, my toothbrush will stand erect to salute you, my beloved hostage. And every night, when you're home from your escapades, I'll hold you captive once more. I'll take the sandals off your feet, for the ground I tread on is holy.

I'll infest your house with paintings and I'll scribble over your decaying walls in rich calligraphy. I'll infuse your bedroom with my perfumed clothes and swollen dreams and the drudgery of my imagination.

Who are you to question my motives?

Who are you to cure my despair or channel my outburst into more creative streams?

I cannot be tamed or trimmed, or cut down to size.

I am larger than life.

I am fierce, violent, resplendent.

Come smell me.

Come watch me burn.

I am combustible.

Flammable.

And I want.

I want. I want. I want.

The 'M' Word

One summer morning during our first year together, I woke up to find your moist body glued to mine. The night had been sultry. I'd shorn off all extraneous layers, had shed my clothes hours before; so when I woke up, my black body was reflecting light.

Half awake, half asleep, still lost in dreams, your fingers wandered across my body like pilgrims in search of the Promised Land, finally arriving at the threshold of my cunt. You lost the battle against sleep. Your now limp fingers bore witness to this defeat. They floated in the wet of my spill. I saved them from drowning. I taught them how to swim, how to tread the waters' depth and stay afloat.

I surprised you with my gesture, rescued you from the snares of sleep. You drew closer, buried your lips in the warm cove where my neck meets my shoulder. I continued to walk your fingers through worlds buried undersea, submerged hallways and ancient palaces. You cast away my grip so your fingers could voyage independently. You travelled through desolate routes, went in circles, but refused to stop to seek instruction. You ambled your way into hidden continents until finally you arrived at the core of my second heart and tampered with its pulse.

You held me as I released that final ounce of breath that would bring me back to the sun-curled morning.

We lay in the speechless afterglow of that self-effacing moment. Your arms encasing me, your mouth drawing in the air from mine as if encroaching on the privacy of my pleasure.

Then, candidly, you opened your mouth, rippling the texture of the stillness.

'What do you think about when you masturbate?'

I remember clearly how you uttered the taboo word, with a stress on the first and last syllable.

What I forget is my reply. It must have been incoherent. I must have been surprised by the forwardness of your question. I wasn't sure if it was designed to invade the secrecy of my fantasies or if it stemmed from your desire for knowledge that was otherwise forbidden.

Later, so I could offer you an answer worthy of your intrusiveness, I sought out the origin of the word and found it was inherently deviant—*manusturprare*, to defile with the hand.

I defile myself regularly. There are days when all I do is lie in bed and defile myself.

Imagine the stark contrast of my ebony fingers nudging against the haughty pink of my cunt; the dialogue I conduct between skin and flesh; the reaching into my cavernous core; the time spent in shameless combustions; the momentary quenching of an eternal thirst.

My fingers serve me best. They are dexterous and adventurous. They know and love the texture of my cunt; the soft, smooth edges of my labia; my perky, elated clit. They know of secret entrances, of shortcuts and escape hatches, of passageways that lead to buried treasure. They are high priests in this Holy Ground, my sanctum sanctorum.

There are days when I drip despite myself as if writing in silent ecstasy. I wake up wanting and cannot shake away the urge to defile myself. My feet guide my body through the restless world of the living, but my thoughts lie suspended in some other ethereal realm. I drip until I start to spill. My nipples are alert and graze against the fabric of my clothes. My pores are receptive to every slight brush of wind. I am all cunt, all receptacle, all slush.

On days like these it is nature that seduces me with her wild scent of laburnum or chameli, or the silly feel of her grass against my bare feet, the fleeting banter of hedonistic pigeons making love in thin air, the cantankerous laughter of fresh, green leaves. I participate in this world outside my body. My surface exterior is deceptively calm. No one would know of the scent of wet earth newly born in my cunt. I tease myself. I continue the charade. I let the spill build into a flood, until I can no longer wait, until I must hurry to my bed and tend to my hysteria.

I use the first three fingers of my right hand, the ones I use to write. My thumb waits outside, by the brink, for fear of drowning. My index finger and the tallest one begin to trace circles outside the mouth of my cunt.

An orgasm is a tangible thrill. Imagine it as clay slowly slipping into being, guided by the contours of fingers held against the sleek, sizzling spin of a potter's wheel, the dizzy circumference churning mud. There is shape-shifting, a delicate rise and fall until the walls evolve, until the reliefs acquire definition; sweeping curves, measured lilt. The peak is that immediate moment when the pot is suddenly complete and is separated from the wheel. Leftover are sighs, then the opening of eyes, the curling of toes, the clasping together of thighs, the return from Wonderland.

Often I read. I lie in bed, let loose my hair, unfasten my clothes, hold a book a few inches away from my face and begin to swallow words. I don't stop to chew, I let them slide along my throat into my belly so they can enter my blood and course through me.

I read Nin, and Winterson. Miller. Anne Carson. Angela Carter's *Black Venus*, Michael Ondantjee's 'Cinnamon Peeler' (*You could never walk through markets / without the profession of my fingers / floating over you*), or recipes by Miss Lawson, or by Laura Esquivel, or Gertrude Stein, who has this to say of 'Roast Beef': *In the inside there is sleeping, in the outside there is reddening, in the morning there is meaning, in the evening there is feeling. Please beef, please beef, pleasure is not wailing. Please beef, please be carved clear, please be a case of consideration,* 'And of Salad Dressing and an Artichoke', *Please pale hot, please cover rose, please acre in the red stranger, please butter all the beefsteak with regular feel faces.*

Words are aphrodisiacs. They evoke the smell and feel of the substances they suggest. They tempt and lure with their promise of tangible things, and of worlds outside of my reach. They inflict me with lust, they fill me with want. Words become substitutes for your touch.

Hell is a world bereft of words. There are days I live through it, when episodes of language lie constrained inside my lungs, when residues float to the surface betraying the script I had in mind. I, the onanist, take shelter in the dark, warm cave of my cunt. I inscribe upon my walls, I make word paintings, I write songs. I scribble at will and colonize every inch of available space. I mark my presence inside my body and listen to the echoes of spoken words. My vagina is the archive of all my greatest works that I can never read.

Sometimes I make love to silence. To elusive, wordless sounds; the interstices between raindrops, or typewriter keys, the pauses in lyrical refrains, the soft gasps of breath between syllables, the lines buried between lines, the vacant silence of vacant hallways, the imagined solitude of abandoned cities, the second-long break between the flapping of bird wings, the hush that follows after bells have tolled, the loneliness of crumpled sheets, the wordlessness of the mute, the grand echoes of mountain passes, the curled silence between the ebbing and flowing of tides, the wisdom of angels and the aftermath of their delirious, choral songs. To these, and more, I come.

I don't wail as I do. I listen to my body gush. My skin quivers, my head stretches away from the rest of me, my feet gasp, my heart beats vociferously, you can feel its raging pulse anywhere you touch, my eyes shut themselves, my lips part; so my mouth is now open and what follows from the bit of my being to the tip of my tongue are cries as delicate and lively as a swarm of butterflies. They flutter by and leave their wings behind.

Sometimes I make love to you. I rummage through memories ... of the first time we fucked on the night we first met. *I couldn't help myself,* you would say later, when I asked you why you did what you did, why you unmasked my body and plunged into my depths. *I wanted you. I had to have you.* You lost your tongue inside my mouth the first time we kissed. I had to remind you of the lateness of the hour, the vanishing of the moon, that I lived in another part of town and had to get home before dawn. How you pinned me against a slice of wall and sprawled your lips against my nipples.

You're not going anywhere. And how you groan when you come, like a warm, suffering thing. Mornings when you hurl your body against me and tweak my nipples like they were switches you could turn on and off. How you lick my teats and kiss my knees, the feel of your beard against my breasts, the hunger in your breath, the scent of sunlight basking on your skin.

Sometimes I recall the taste of you in long-drawn moments with my mouth between your legs. You close your eyes and lie still and erect. I wet you with kisses, then lick you with my tongue until you start to spill. I make all kinds of patterns against the blackboard of your skin. I draw you in and out. I place you deep inside my throat as if I were swallowing you whole. You gasp and stretch and clasp my hair with your fingers. I plunge forward and retreat, repeatedly, in a soothing spree. You relent. You feed me all there is to feed. You are a secret recipe, one I can never untangle with my tongue; such perfection of taste, such exacting proportion of salt to spice, such delicate consistency.

Sometimes I make love to this city under the cover of the open sky. I cocoon myself in the cool breath of the evening sun. Trees glisten, flowers prepare to close for the night. Amid forsaken rooftops, birds take flight for a final search of scattered grain, some swoop against the tops of trees and make vertiginous circles in the air. I too take flight. I begin my ascent towards dizzying peaks, altitudes I could never surmount with my bare feet. I traipse along the outskirts of the aether, I touch the voluptuous flesh of clouds, I submit to the burning skin of evening stars.

An Ex-lover's Discourse

He slips into the dressing gown suspended from the hook of the coat stand that is part of the minimal mis-en-scène. He settles into the chair placed on stage for him, reaches for the hot water bottle resting inches away on a stool like a prop. Finally, with the air of an aristocrat, he pours himself a glass of Scotch. Words fall into place: the anonymous quote on the invite—*A dressing gown, a hot water bottle and some whisky, if you can procure it, are really all you need. They are the absolute essentials for a writer.*

If only that were true.

There isn't a single vacant stretch of space. The audience spills over, the exits have to be unlocked to contain the crowd of listeners and worshippers. I park myself on a step that is a member of the staircase that connects the stage to the exit like a clogged artery. I'm here on a one-point agenda; to have him inscribe his signature on my copy of his book, a pocket-sized collection of fables gifted to me by an ex-lover.

In between silences, I peep into the first page and re-read the dedication:

Ms Chocolate Truffle,

Gardez en memoire les moments que nous avons passé ensemble. Continuez d'ecrire. Je croire en vous. Julien. (Preserve the moments we have spent together. Continue to write. I believe in you. Julien.)

You can't but appreciate the choice of words, his attempt to downplay our intimacy. *Gardez,* he wrote, using the imperative. It must share roots with the word 'guard'.

He loosens the dressing gown and after fielding several questions is too fatigued to continue the conversation. The crowd begins to shuffle towards the exit. I hurry instead to the foot of the stage, draw his attention and place the book in his hands.

'Should I address it to you?' he asks politely.

'If you want to. It doesn't matter, really,' I assure him.

He opens the book, like etiquette demands, to arrive at the page on which he would have to sign after carefully crossing off the printed version of his name. But he stumbles instead upon the page that bears the ex-lover's inscription.

'This is a revelation,' he says.

'An ex-lover,' I explain.

'There'll be others.'

'There already are.'

({})

I've never cared much for labels. In fact, the first thing I do after I've bought a brand new dress is rip off the tiny strip of cloth that's attached to the back of the collar. It makes me itch, or pops out at the wrong times to reveal too much and signify too little. Even my kitchen shelves are lined with bottles I've rescued from the imprisoning arms of paper labels.

I prefer ambiguity.

Given my disdain for categories, I find myself struggling for a term that would adequately describe all the men who've ventured inside the folds of my body. The momentary men, the beads on my rosary of conquests, the subjects of my dated affairs; these one- and two- and three-night stands that meant everything and nothing; the ones I was careful not to fall in love with for fear of interfering with the intimacy of the immediate.

Would it be inappropriate to refer to them as lovers?

A lover is one who loves in ways that are yet to be anthologized.

An ex-lover is one who has had the privilege of having once been my lover.

I keep returning to Botton, whose words I've scribbled out on a scrap of paper and blue-tacked to the wall beside my bed. It's an excerpt from *The Romantic Movement*. To date I cannot say for sure whether I agree with his philosophy or am vehemently opposed to it. *To go to bed with another is in some way to collide with the memories and habits of all those they have ever been with. Our way of making love embodies the mnemonic of our sexual history, a kiss is an enriched model of past kisses, our behaviour in the bedroom filled with traces of past bedrooms in which we have slept.*

I've always approached my lovers as present-tense beings. Each unique in matters of the body, each with their own philosophy of lips and touch, each an individual adventure with a different plotline. At best, I see them as fragments of a patchwork quilt held together by delicate threads.

You **do not** belong to this tapestry.
Not yet.

({})

J was a sleep-fucker.

Our affair was brief. I met him four years ago, just a few days before I was to leave University to return to my city-by-the-sea, in keeping with my rule of meeting at least one person on the brink of departure who I could regret not having encountered before.

We met at a house party where he spent all evening circling around my periphery, dipping in now and then to incite me with some callous comment or a suggestive statement or with his quick-witted touch. He had a presence about him that stemmed from pride. He could disarm and destroy you with his charm. That's what he did during the course of that first evening; he whetted my appetite, and when I was ready to indulge, withdrew the feast. I spent more time there than I wanted to, looking for scraps to chew on. He turned indifferent. So I went up to him to say goodbye.

'I'm sure we'll see each other again,' he said.

'I doubt it,' I said. 'I'm leaving the city in less than a week.' I hoped at least now he might understand the urgency of this passion.

'Well, too bad,' were his last words.

So I found him online and explained to him I didn't have time to play. We fixed a date.

We watched a Bollywood flick at a shady cinema hall in RK Puram. A deliberate choice. Multiplexes are too mainstream.

He's French but his Hindi is impeccable; not once did I need to translate a thing. We watched the film obediently, with controlled abandon, in the darkness of the hall. Not once did he lean across to touch me or have his hands callously graze against mine. He's much too proud to make the first move. He'd rather I relented, surrendered gracefully to my lust. The credits rolled, we exited reluctantly, then walked the length of the road like two restless travellers afraid to go home. We found a brick wall around the corner of the street and parked ourselves there and continued to talk. He told me about his cat, his home in Chantilly, his ex-lovers, and finally, his inability to engross himself in 'casual flings'. Later I would remind him of his reluctance. 'What makes you think this is a casual fling?' he would reply.

Hours passed. The sky broke down like it is wont to do in the peak of summer. But we didn't care to honour the downpour. We continued to feast on conversation showed no concern for time and going well past 2 a.m.

His body was still too separate from mine. It had been three hours since we began and he hadn't shown any signs of surrender.

I can't remember much more of the conversation, all I know is that just when I doubted his intentions, the mosquitoes surfaced. They started to nibble at the flesh around my calves, my feet, and my neck. I'd carelessly slipped on a thin, flair cotton skirt before our date. I didn't have time to take a shower and get dressed. Just an hour before, I'd been with another lover, T.

I continued to listen and listening still, reached into my jhola and fished out the roll-on repellent I carried with me at all times; a gift from the Swede. Without interrupting his monologue, I uncorked the repellent and rolled the ball against the surface of my calf and the insides of my thighs. When I looked up to punctuate the conversation with a random reply, I found him transfixed.

I decided it's time I returned to university. It's the end of the semester; I'd got papers overdue. We walked towards an auto, negotiated a price. The driver revved the accelerator. I slid closer and pressed my lips against his. We kissed.

He lived just outside campus. But he was unwilling to escort me back home. He said he would if we first dropped by his place and had a drink. Old Monk is all he had. I willingly relented. We went upstairs.

In the five nights that followed, I discovered his sleep-fucking quirk. After the final moan, the twilight sigh, I'd fall asleep naked beside him. He had no bed, just a mattress on the floor. I'd be busy rummaging through dreams as I am inclined to do in the middle of sleephood until I'd slip out of sleep to find his lips burried in the niche between my neck and my collarbone. His body would rise to greet me. His pack of rubber was always kept strategically below the mattress. I began to understand why. Half-awake, half-asleep, he'd enter me lightly and cocoon himself until I took flight.

({})

A week before J, I'd had my first brush with the Turk who redefined 'cocky'. We had known each other before, had exchanged wit on several occasions, but had our first serious conversation at the same party where I'd encountered him. We spoke for hours, it seemed, until a French woman threw a tantrum because the Turk wasn't paying her any attention. I left with T, the Turk tagged along, and we began our walk from Munirka to campus. Home was closer for T and me, our hostels only a kilometre away from the gate.

The Turk lived in Brahmaputra Extension, the hostel at the end of the universe.

So I lent him the keys to my bicycle. And then didn't hear from him for at least twenty-four hours, during which I had been liaising with T.

It was a beautiful bicycle, a Hercules racing bike. Tall and gorgeous, just like A, the lover who'd left it for me when he'd returned to his country.

I resorted to email, the subject-line brief and stately: 'Bicycle Thief'.

I offered to visit him at Brahmaputra to pick up the bicycle.

His reply was unprecedented.

You can't just come and pick up your bike like that! If I was that simple, life would have been easier for many people. Come and we can decide on the terms.

Obviously, I had to go.

I knock on the door and find it is ajar. He tells me to come in. I do and find him busy at his desk, cigarette in hand, a can of beer on the table.

'You're late,' he says as he turns to acknowledge my presence.

I examine his room. There are posters on the wall, of consciously tacky, 'exotic' things, there's a mosquito net spread across his bed like a veil, a map of Delhi taped against the wall beside his desk, and in one corner, an ice bucket filled with cans of beer. I help myself to some beer and sit on the edge of his bed.

'Did you really think it would be that simple? You'd come here, I'd treat you to chai and then you'd leave with your cycle?' he says.

Before I can answer, he turns to his desk, retrieves my keys from under his laptop and places them on the desk, and gestures at me to examine them.

'I could just take the key and go away. There's no need for formalities.'

'You can if you want to.'

I reach out for the keys and hold them between my fingers. I make as if to leave, then sit down again.

'You're right, it shouldn't be so easy.'

'So when do I get to read the erotica?'

'Why would you want to?'

'I'd like to know if it's any good! This would be the perfect setting for a brand-new piece. I'm sure that's why you came.'

'Don't flatter yourself.'

So I find something online that I'd written for a magazine. He sits on the floor right beside my feet. I read him something called 'Lost and Found'.

When I finish, I return to my seat on the edge of his bed. He moves from the floor to the chair, which he brings closer to the bed. I lie down, mischievously, a Freudian slip. I'm now on the 'couch'. He starts to interrogate me about my life, my work. I indulge him. I divulge.

Beer makes me pissy. I leave the room and turn the lights off on the way out so that the room is only half-lit by his study lamp.

When I return, I walk towards him, kiss him, then move away.

'Now we have to pretend that didn't happen.'

'Why?'

'Because I'd like to have several first kisses, and I don't want you to stop talking.'

We couldn't pretend. What followed was the slow unravelling

of clothes, breaths between kisses, an emergency, an urgent need to conquer and be conquered, then surrender.

I wake up to the feeling of cold metal against my navel. Bicycle keys.

He's sitting beside me. He offers a smile.

'You demolished my room.'

I look around. The mosquito net had fallen apart, the poster near the bed had come undone, the carpets have been tossed to the edges of the room.

'I apologize. I doubt I'll come again.'

'Well, the next time you "don't come", could you wear a skirt?'

'Why should I return?'

'Because I got a very raw deal?'

'What do you mean?'

'Well, I just lost a bicycle!'

({})

Fifty-four wooden blocks, each three times as long as it is wide, each one-fifth as thick as it is long. Three blocks are stacked at the base, to form a level on which seventeen levels of three blocks each are placed adjacent to each other, along their long side, perpendicular to the previous level, to form a wooden tower.

He was a random acquaintance who'd charmed me into inviting him over to my terrace. Above us, only the naked night illuminated by stars. I'm in no mood for conversation, so I suggest we play a game of Jenga. I erect the tower upon the wobbly table, place a chair on either side, invite him to take a seat. The stakes are unstated. I place one hand firmly against the table, to urge it into standing upright, to fix the quirky wobble. I make the first move, retrieve a block from the centre of the third layer and place it on the top-most level as the rules dictate.

Only one hand at a time may be used to remove a block. Either hand can be used, but only one hand is allowed to be in contact with the tower at any given point.

I avoid eye contact, keep my gaze firmly on the looming tower. I can sense his eyes travelling across my body, peering through the cloth of my dress. I say nothing.

Jenga isn't the only game we're playing.

Ten moves later, the tower is still in place. He's about to make his move, I lift my eyes and watch him as his fingers tug at a tight block. He manages to dislodge it and places it on the top. The tower is much taller now and it blocks his view of me. I can no longer gauge his intentions. Right then, I feel the sweep of his fingers against my stationary left hand. He knows I cannot draw it away because if I do, the game will end. And the trick to Jenga, like with seduction, is to prolong the inevitable, to stretch the moment as infinitely as possible before the unravelling. The tauter the stretch, the stronger the intensity, the deeper the passion.

He makes patterns against my arms, then moves suavely across the canvas of my shoulders. I remain speechless. There's no need for language.

Carefully, without upsetting the alignment of the table, he wraps his feet around my feet. His toes probe the texture of my skin. I feel the trickle inside me, my body has begun the process of meltdown, the weight of the tower starts to shift towards one side. Any moment now, it will collapse.

The rules dictate that the game ends when the tower falls in even a minor way or if there is a significant collapse where the tower crumbles exposing the base. However, if one or more blocks fall, but all players agree that they can be put back on the tower for play to resume, that is in keeping with the spirit of the game.

We persist. We continue to cast block against block, level against level, but the tower's lower half is beginning to relent, it's only a matter of seconds before it all falls down.

By now I'm ready to surrender. Now and then, between the blocks, I glimpse his gorgeous brown skin. I trace, with my eyes, the sharp outline of his face, the swell of his lips, the lure of his gaze. The brush-strokes continue, except his hand is no longer on mine, his fingers traipse along my thighs and venture further, deeper until he confronts the source of my lust.

Suddenly, I can't see him on the other side, he seems to have disappeared. Then I feel the clean sweep of his tongue against my clit.

I play my last move. There are too many spaces between the blocks. For a second the tower stands tall. Then, just as his tongue makes butterfly strokes against my clit, the blocks collapse and spill over to the ground.

No Sex Again Last Night

I haven't exactly been keeping track. I don't strike lines against a wall nor do I tally them to study their steady increase. It's purely incidental how I arrived at this nondescript bit of trivia. I happened to retrace my footsteps and suddenly stumbled upon the last time we happened to fuck. At last count, it was two hundred and forty-six days ago.

I can't be sure how many of these two hundred and forty-six days you've spent away from this city, wanderlusting on account of work, crisscrossing continents to document lives. I cannot even say for sure how many of these nights were spent in the same city and under the same sheets.

What I do know for certain is that there was never any dearth of opportunity.

Like those summer nights when in the agony of heat, in the middle of my sleep, I'd take off my shirt to expose myself to fleeting sighs of wind; sheetless nights when the fan was all whir and no whirl; powerless nights when the air conditioner went off with a whimper; shirtless nights with skin pressed against bare skin, the sudden surprise of my nipples against your shoulder blades; sunburnt mornings emblazoned by light when you'd wake up and take shelter under me as if I were a tall, leaf-filled tree; monsoon nights when it rained so hard we had to seal the windows, and still the scent of wet earth would seep in and enchant us until we fell asleep under its spell and we'd wake up intoxicated with lust. I'd be as wet as a puddle. All you had to do was jump in and swirl. But you wouldn't and I couldn't imagine why; winter nights when we'd cling to each other for warmth, your feet entwined within mine, my arms wrapped around you like a shawl. Foggy, frosty mornings when all I wanted was your body, hot and warm and firm inside me.

It was you who initiated me into the pleasures of morning sex. You taught me to anticipate the sun. You steered me into a pattern and soon I learned to dedicate the evening to food and wine and song, and to spend the night in a state of want.

And right on cue, as the sky shed shades, you'd release me from my state of sleephood and enter.

In these eight months you've managed to meddle with our carefully crafted script. I no longer know my lines and I've forgotten what role I'm expected to play. Am I the seductress or the seduced?

Every morning I wake up hoping you will finally quench this now centuries-old thirst. But you draw me close, kiss my mouth repeatedly and then quietly make your exit from the landscape of the bedroom. And so everyday I nurse this lust. I pet it, soften it, temper it. And yet, every night it grows in size and strength.

({})

I hold you responsible for having aroused in me, through this extended foreplay, something more vital than passion, something elemental and irrepressible; a bottomless hunger that can no longer be fed away. If you were unfeeling and cruel, if you had another lover who consumed your body, if you were no longer chemically attracted to me, I would understand. But each night you bury your face within my breasts, you caress my aching body with the wisdom of a healer, you feel for my heartbeat and you let me study yours when you park your lust right beside mine so I can feel you growing in size and strength.

I could seduce you. I've thought about it. I could impose my lips on your body, make you swell with hunger and desire. I could appeal to your mouth. I could parade my nakedness, make you yearn for me.

But I refuse to.

I want *you* to finish what *you* started.

Unfurl me like a daydream. Touch my sweet and luscious core. I reek of spring and holy things and I taste like evening.

({})

At 12.30 p.m. this afternoon, I bid you goodbye. You were on your way to the airport. I'd helped you pack, had rid the fridge of all things cursed with a short shelf span, had ironed your Nehru coats so you could wear one at the lecture you were slated to present in the land of our former colonizer. We held hands in the taxi. We snuck our private gesture behind our handbags so the driver wouldn't be witness to our intimacy.

Eight hours later, I'm slipping into a summer dress, trying to disguise my reluctance. I'm not sure why I agreed to reacquaint myself with L, a man I'd spent one night with sometime last year when you were away. He happens to be in town for a few hours and he's intent on seeing me again.

I contemplate faking a last-minute illness. I can predict the flow of our conversation and I know he would like it to end with me poised beneath him. I was sure I didn't want to go there. Not again.

I repress the urge to curse you. I'm still upset about the other night when I was about to collapse into the welcoming arms of sleep. You came to bed later and wound your legs strategically so your feet lay pressed against my cunt.

'Are you fast asleep?' you asked.

'What do you want?'

'Could you please press the tips of my toes?'

'Do I have a choice?'

I pressed the little gaps between your toes, then pulled at their tips. When you were satisfied, you turned your back to me and asked me to relieve you of the itch on your back.

I felt sympathy. You are allergic to so many things and this past week the skin on your back had broken into a rash and I couldn't even begin to imagine how frustrating it must have been for you to not be able to reach the regions that itched most. I scratched your back. You purred like a tomcat.

Then you buried your head in your pillow and were about to break into sleep.

'That's what I've become,' I said. 'Backscratcher and masseuse.'

'What do you mean?' you asked.

'You see me as a spare set of hands. I have a body too,' I said.

'Well, I've told you before; consider finding a younger lover, someone who can satisfy you.'

At which point I succumbed to my angry pose and turned against your body, slipped into a corner and threatened to sleep without kissing you goodnight.

But I relented.

'You deserve to be satisfied,' you added.

'It isn't about satisfaction,' I replied.

'Then what is it about?'

'Touch. It's about touch. You used to touch me in a certain way and you don't anymore,' I said as I uncoiled myself from the fetal position I'd assumed and lay flat on my back, my palms spread against my head.

'You mean like this?' and you encased my fingers within your fingers so your pulse could invade my own.

By then, despite the current that passed through me, a tear coursed past my cheek.

I waited for the surge to subside and when I was sure you had passed into sleep, released my fingers from the bondage of your 'touch', turned around and tried to negotiate my passage through the underground of sleep.

When I woke up the next morning I could taste the anger on my tongue. As is my style, I said nothing. I answered your every remark with a monosyllabic smile. It took three such instances for you to finally catch on.

'Are you pissed off?' you asked at last.

'No. Not at all,' I said faking reassurance.

You didn't pursue the matter, went for a walk instead and asked me to make you a bowl of porridge for breakfast.

When you returned, you noticed my face was still twisted in the shape of a grimace. So you did that corny thing you do where you smile at me patronizingly and expect that like a monkey, I'll mimic your smile and erase my frown.

It didn't work.

'I guess I am pissed at you,' I revealed, finally.

'Why? What did I do this time?' you asked most innocently.

'It's okay, fuck it.'

'No, tell me.'

'You insulted me last night.'

'How?'

'By suggesting I take on a younger lover.'

'But I've said that to you before too, it can't possibly have come as a surprise.'

'That's the thing! After everything we've been through, you're still suggesting I take a lover.'

'I'm sorry. I'll take that back.'

'You should. It's disrespectful.'

'I'm sorry.'

'It's just that before, you used to touch me in a certain way, and I find, increasingly, that you don't. You want me instead to administer to your aches and itches.'

'I'm sorry.'

Later, when I was scrubbing the dishes, you snuck up behind me and put your lips to my neck and your fingers against my crotch. I turned to liquid, my body smouldered in the warmth of your breath.

'Hmmm ... Don't touch me like that,' I said teasingly.

'Oh really?'

'No. Don't not touch me like that!'

Despite that make-up touch, I'm still pissed off at you for

your suggestion, and for having generally reduced me to a Lady-Macbeth-like caricature. Each time I make love to another, I find I wash myself repeatedly until all traces of digression have been shaken off and my body is a blank slate once again, clear and vacant enough for you to write anew upon my skin.

This wouldn't have happened if you had enforced monogamy. If you had laid down rules and asked me to abide by them. But you don't care for cuckoldry. You don't care for possession. You prefer to let me make my own rules, be with whomever I wish.

The ex used to say the same thing, except he'd make too much of a grand gesture out of 'giving me' my freedom, 'Your body doesn't belong to me,' he would say. 'You have every right to be with whomever you want,' he'd add. 'Just don't tell me about it, I don't think I want to know.' I was young then, even younger than I am now. And as long as he was around, I never faltered, never indulged in other bodies. But when he left this city of djinns, during my second year of University, things fell apart. I discovered the world of men, and the thrill of conquest.

I assumed the role of picara and made my way through the landscape of lust and desire. I never sought out lovers; they just seemed to find their way into my body. The structure was common to all: first the sighting, then the pursuit, which was almost always literary, followed by contact, followed by words. Yes, men made for good muses. Sometimes I couldn't tell if my writing depended on adventure, or if the adventure was incumbent in order for me to write.

({})

As I line my eyes with kohl, infuse my body with mild perfume, and examine my face in the mirror, I'm overwhelmed by how much things have changed. The ex is now married and recently had a baby girl. We don't talk anymore. He couldn't forgive my many 'betrayals'. He didn't really expect I'd make use of the 'freedom' he so patronizingly bestowed on me. He was trying to appeal to my feminist sensibilities. He took my infidelities personally. I could separate love and sex, he couldn't. He knew, also, we would never be equals, that I would always be more easily desired than he, a socially awkward, overweight, boyish economist with a noticeably receding hairline.

I wondered then, as I wonder now, what it was that I sought in past lovers. Was it the lure of a good story, or the thrill of seducing and being seduced, or was it just a phase in my life, a transition I was trying to make from girlhood to womanhood? Or was I searching for fragments of myself?

I know for certain that desire was at the root of this search. I enjoyed being pursued, an indulgence I had never known as young girl. I loved waking up in a bed not my own. I delighted in the power of my body. I revelled in the company of men and found strange comfort in the transience of the moment.

You, too, were supposed to be a one-night stand. A quick fix. A conquest. A ten-line poem in my grand anthology of lovers.

But you altered the narrative, you marked your territory on my timeline so that as I look back, I find I can neatly divide my more recent past into two unequal halves: before you and after.

({})

It was a few months into our acquaintance when my body first began to betray me.

I find it ironic, in retrospect, that the lover in question who was privy to this first bodily deceit was a sculptor.

We'd seen each other at a few art openings. At some point he asked for my number and a few days later, invited me to his studio for dinner. He promised me fish curry, Kerala-style, in keeping with his origins. I agreed.

He lived in the other end of the city. I had to take a train. His studio was reasonably spacious, finished paintings leaned against the walls. We talked over several refills of Old Monk. I cannot remember the contents of our dialogue. It must have been inconsequential. Sufficiently high, we decided it was time for dinner.

He led me to his kitchen and let me take in the scent of the fish curry. While I was at it, I deftly surveyed his body. His muscles were firm and taut, his skin supple, impressive for a man past forty. It was the yoga, he told me later. He was a few inches taller than I; still he seemed to tower above me. I wasn't quite sure why I was there. I have a vague recollection of wanting to prove to myself that I wasn't attached to you, that I was a free bird whose wings you dared not clip.

The sculptor was now a breath away. I leaned against the kitchen wall and ran my coy fingers through my hair. I may have taken in a long sip of air, may possibly have closed my eyes. When I was done with my sensuous appreciation of the promising curry, I found him pressed against my body, his lips about to make dialogue with mine, until suddenly he had begun to mould me with his fingers. Before I could react, he began to take off my clothes.

He raised me on my toes, swung one arm against the back of my thighs and lifted me to his makeshift bed. He lay upon me and positioned my body strategically so he could steal into me in the darkness. He began to fill my body's hollow with repeated strokes and showed no signs of ceasing.

'You're strong,' he said.

He fucked me just the way I like being fucked, no delicate twists and turns, no gentle caresses, hard, definite reaching in and out with the certainty of destination.

It was sometime around my fifth little death that I felt the first drop of salt. It had yet to make its way past my lower eyelid, but it foretold an impending flood. It was my first lesson in body dichotomy; the paradox of pleasure coupled with misery. It was my first betrayal in which my body desired to be with a body other than the one it was with.

I pulled myself together and played my move and led the sculptor into well-earned delight. I waited the customary five minutes during which his heart tried hard to relax its furious beating. Then I left him to lie on the belly of the mattress as I made my way to the bathroom.

Once in, I locked the door, looked into the mirror, and wept.

My messages to you that night were pathetic. I cannot remember their contents, but they were despicably melancholic. You were already asleep, but you called the next morning.

'What was that about?' you asked.

'What do you mean?'

'Your messages last night, what was that about?'

'Oh. I was having a bad night. I didn't mean to bother you.'

'It obviously came from somewhere. What's up?'

'It was just this sudden realization I had, that if you and I had to fall apart, if I were to leave you, it wouldn't make any difference to your life.'

'Well, it's just not that kind of relationship.'

'I guess it isn't. I don't know why I thought it was.'

({})

It's 8 p.m. I promised L that I would meet him at 8.30 p.m. for dinner. He wanted to eat at the same place we dined at last year, when we met. I agreed. I confront my bathroom mirror for a final glance and am taken aback by how much I've aged since I first met you. I'm not as vulnerable as I was then. There are strands of grey sprouting between my otherwise jet-black locks. I've taken to wearing earrings, an accessory I didn't much care for before. But this is a nice, casual pair; they dangle from my earlobes and almost touch my shoulders.

I have a strange feeling in the pit of my belly, something akin to impending doom, and it makes me rethink my decision to meet L. But it's too late to cancel. He doesn't have a phone, and I'm not cruel enough to stand him up. I dab perfume on my wrists and behind my ears, take a deep breath and find my way to the door.

Half an hour later, I spot him walking the streets of Hauz Khas Village. He spots me too and his gait quickens with anticipation. He holds me tight when he sees me and as soon as we get into a darker alley, he pins me against a wall and kisses me with authority, empties a year's lust into a few stop-motion minutes. I receive his kiss although my mind has already left my body. I'm a mere puppet now, passive against his desire.

I feel unclean.

'You can do this.' My vacant brain cells send half-hearted signals to the rest of my body that's already beginning to resist this onslaught of passion. I break away from his embrace and lead him to the chosen restaurant. He follows obediently, trying hard to disguise the bulge of his hardened flesh.

As we wait for our drinks to arrive, we catch up on a year's worth of news. He's doing well, will soon be delivering lectures at Princeton, his stint in Afghanistan continues to bode well, he's been travelling the world since I last saw him, but he keeps revisiting that one night we spent together.

It was almost exactly a year ago. I met him through a friend at some art do. We'd got along instantly. There was a nakedness to his intent; his desire for me was obvious within the first few minutes of our exchange. We'd headed back to my one-room barsati and decided we'd cook pasta. He was beautiful in the kitchen, he took charge of the inner lives of tomatoes and garlic, boiled the pasta to *al dente* imperfection, and within minutes we were ready to eat. We talked while we applied finishing touches to our meal. I can't remember what was said but at some point, while my hand held a knife that dripped tomato blood, he drew my face to his and kissed me on my mouth. We didn't eat that night. He lured me to my bedroom, undid my clothes and caressed every inch of me. I didn't resist. You had been away then for such a long time, there was an ache inside of me that he promised to remedy. We fucked. Once was all I could muster. By now I was already trying to resist the impulse to leave the bed and take a shower so I could wash off the indulgence. I finally did. I drenched my body in cold water and soaped each part of me till I felt clean again and then returned to him, my hair dripping wet. He welcomed me with restless fingers.

'I need to sleep,' I said.

'I understand,' he said.

'Tomorrow is a really long day.'

'I can imagine,' he said as he speckled my face with soft tiny kisses.

I turned off the lights and tried to bury myself in his embrace, but his body kept betraying him; it wouldn't soften despite my attempts at sleep. So I lay a few inches aside in the hope that the distance would do him some good. It did, eventually. He fell asleep. I lay awake for hours, my gaze fixed on the whir of the fan.

({})

To be honest, I was afraid. You were always away. And I didn't know what to do with all my lust. If only there was some way I could have emptied myself, relinquished my connection with you. Sometimes I wondered if all I'd known since I met you was the pain of suffering; the kind of suffering that can only find absolution through indulgence, through the exercise of desire.

So, instead of listening to the moral of my body's betrayal, I decided to put it to the test. I chose to submit myself to other passions. I willed my mind to quell its hesitations and threw myself headlong into desire. I decided to surrender to the game of seduction in the hope that I would find resolution for my addiction to you. There was every possibility that in the course of my infidelities, I would find someone better than you, younger than you, more suited to my temperament. It had become imperative that I demystify you. It was my only hope for salvation.

There were others I coveted momentarily, and then wished they would leave me alone after the deed was done. I didn't fancy having to share my bed. I couldn't sleep when there was company. Not because I was too full of lust but because my body didn't know how to shapeshift, how to mould itself against their bodies, how to relent and submit to the softness of post-coital drowsiness.

You are responsible for this insatiable hunger. You regularly invite me to feast at your table and when I'm ready to eat, refuse to feed me. Instead, you let me indulge this insatiable hunger, this irredeemable thirst. I suffer in your presence and in your absence. When you return from your journeying I know you will collect all your tiredness and collapse in my arms, unleash the bulk of your accumulated sleep, and the next night and the night after, you will continue to tease my lust without acknowledging it.

({})

L wants me. And although my body doesn't respond to him instinctively, it yields to his aggressive touch. We've ordered our meal and he steals glances at me as he fills me in on his one-year absence. We talk about pre-historic art, eighteenth-century Persian erotica, in between he even recites a Persian poem, which he then translates for me, though I cannot remember what it said. I was worried about how to dodge the midnight kiss, the prelude to the otherwise inevitable. When food was placed on the table, he took care to serve me first, the way you always do. I ate, though I wasn't hungry. I swallowed multiple glasses of beer. Intoxication, I decided, would be my redemption. As the evening continued and we progressed to dessert, I was reasonably inebriated. I could feel the onslaught of courage coursing through my blood.

'So must you really go back to work on your book?' he asked, finally.

'I really must,' I said. 'But even if I didn't have to, I don't think we can repeat last year's adventure.'

'Why not? It was so beautiful. I've thought of you so much.'

'To be honest, I just find I'm unable to engage with another body. I'm obsessed with my lover's body, even though he hardly indulges mine.'

'Maybe it's because you're in love with him?'

'I am, but that had never stopped me in the past. In my first relationship, for instance.'

'Maybe you're growing older.'

'I don't know. It's frustrating. He won't have me and although he says I have every right to be with whoever I want—and he means it—I find myself unable to.'

'Is it guilt?'

'No. I don't feel guilty. I just feel removed ... I can lose myself in another, but only for a few seconds, after which my body is completely conscious that this is not the lover's body, it's an alien form, and then it all descends into chaos. I finish what I've started, but I feel unclean. So I try not to start anything anymore. I think it's because my lover starves me. Sometimes when he's fallen asleep, I cover him with a sheet, kiss his forehead to make sure he's lost in dreams; then I turn to the side and masturbate.'

'When was the last time you were with somebody other than him?'

'A few days ago. He was beautiful. After we were done, I felt satisfied but discontent ... What if my body is just obsessed with him? What if it's because he deprives me of sex? What if it's because I enjoy the slow, steady combustion, because it means I'm perpetually in heat, because it makes me feel so alive and sensuous. What if the Buddha got it all wrong? What if suffering is the root of all desire?'

He smiled at my now-breathless body, slipped his fingers underneath mine and said nothing.

We were the last to leave the restaurant. As we descended the first flight of stairs, he drew me to a corner and ravished my lips and the borders of my collarbone. I indulged him for a few seconds and then drew away. I was in heat but I didn't want him to quell the flames. He understood. He drew his fingers across my face, tucked loose strands of hair behind my ears, then moved closer so his mouth now hovered over my ear.

'Whatever you decide, promise me, whatever you do, you don't lose your passion, that spark you have that makes you you.'

I promised.

({})

Fifteen days later you returned, just like you'd promised. This time your house wasn't a mess. We met that evening. I came over and cooked dinner. You opened a bottle of bourbon you'd picked up, duty-free. We talked, slipped from one revelation to another. I filled you in on a friend's messy courtship—she decided to pursue it, despite knowing that the man she loved could hurt her in unimaginable ways.

'Why doesn't she leave him? Can't she see he's not good enough?'

'She tried to, but she slipped and they got back together. When I asked her why, she quoted Pascal: *Love has reasons of which reason knows naught*. I believe her. She loves him. She sees that there's more to him than he himself is able to fathom. She can't seem to live with him and can't seem to do without him either. Besides, once you start to care for someone, it's hard to suddenly cease. It's a trap.'

'Are we trapped too?'

'What makes you think we are?' I said.

'Well, what if that friend of yours is right? Was it she who said you were giving me your best years?'

'I'm surprised you remember that.'

'Of course I do. And it's true, you're so young, and I'm old. You have so much living left to do whereas I've done my fair share. And as much as I can feel your passion everyday, my tired, ageing body with all its aches and pains doesn't always allow me to respond. And that isn't fair to you, is it?'

'This isn't about sex. It is and it isn't. And I've made my peace with that.'

'I don't want you to be making such huge sacrifices for me. I've been in relationships where I've been the one sacrificing and in others where I've been on the receiving end of a sacrifice and it always ends in resentment. That's the reason why I've been telling you to consider taking on a younger lover.'

'Sometimes it feels as though it's all or nothing with you. You're so stubborn, you're so unwilling to yield.'

'Sweets, if there is one person in my entire life to whom I have yielded, it is you!'

'You think I haven't tried? It's not so simple,' I said.

'I know you've been with many men before me. I don't want to be unfair to you. I am aware of your sexuality. You are so attuned to your body. Like I said, it's not that I don't feel your passion, I feel it all the time. I'm just too exhausted to respond.'

'Well, I'm done with all that. I've been hurt by men because I haven't been willing to give you up. Besides, I've had my fair share of lovers. There was a time when it had its thrill. It felt good to be desired by strangers. But I've had my fill. I don't think I can go through with it again. As you grow older, you realize the things that you did in the heat of the moment no longer satisfy. All the old insecurities I had about my body have dissipated. There's no reason for conquest anymore. Sex is no longer a necessity.'

'Okay...'

'Besides, when you come to bed at night and you hold me, kiss me, stroke my back with your fingers, my body becomes a furnace. You arouse me like no other man has, and so consistently. No one has ever had that effect on me. And instead of that feeling diminishing over time, it has only become more fertile. When you touch me I feel like I'm home. And I no longer want. I suffer, but I no longer suffer.'

You nodded and contined looking at me across the table, and I returned your gaze.

({})

That night you performed the usual ritual when you entered the sheets, kissed me on my lips, wrapped your legs within mine as your fingers made long strokes along the length of my back, moving from the depressed curves of my shoulder blades to the base of my torso. My head lay near your chest and I overheard your heart, first keeping time, then pacing furiously, as if longing to be stilled.

I couldn't resist the impulse. My fingers began to dance over your chest, circling over little moles and soft hairs until, like wild drunks, they toppled over your belly, landing at the seat of your lust.

There they hesitated, unsure whether to proceed with their revelry or return to their senses. You intervened, enabling their insobriety. It was your hand that led mine over your crotch in time to contain the rising of your flesh. I released my body from the clutch of your embrace and, resting on my knees, lowered myself under the cover of your sheets. My mouth was now positioned such that my lips could pout over your foreskin. I feasted on you like an impoverished lover unsure of the timeliness of her next meal, relishing each serving as if attempting to satisfy a delirious, eternal, unfathomable hunger. But you stopped me short seconds before I was about to finish. You beckoned me towards you, your hands grabbing my ass firmly. Then you undressed me. I followed suit and undid your clothes. You held my naked, starving body against your own so I could feel the warmth of your skin invading my own, so I could smell your appetite. You lay me flat on my back and crouched over me, and as you reached for the condom on the cupboard next to the bed, I touched the bits of moonlight trapped within your beard. You knelt over and kissed my knees, causing me to arch my body like a well-feted cat. You raised me higher, the base of your palm elevating my ass. Then you slipped inside me and made up for lost time.

The Poetics of Sleep

There's a story by Jeanette Winterson about a land where sleep is contraband because it decreases productivity. All public spaces are designated 'non-sleeping' areas, and anyone caught in the act of sleep is liable to pay a fine of fifty pounds. Beds may be bought but the mattress must have an in-built alarm clock. If you get caught on a 'bed-check' with a dead alarm, there's another fifty-pound fine. Three fines and you are disqualified from sleeping for a year. The protagonist is one of the very few who are legally permitted to sleep, he's a civil servant though his official designation is 'Dreamer'. When the no-sleep lifestyle was pioneered, it was soon discovered that people functioned better if they had a dream boost. The Dreamer dreams the dreams that constitute the dream boost. He's perhaps the only citizen with a real antique bed who is allowed to sleep for nine to ten hours a day. He could easily be the luckiest man in that sleep-deprived land. And yet, he's the loneliest. Each time he meets a woman his most immediate question is 'Sleep with me?' To which the likeliest reply is, 'You mean lie awake with you? Everybody wants to know if we're lying awake together.'

({})

I don't like to sleep alone. I used to, before I knew the joy of sleeping with you. It isn't sex that complicated things; it's the poetic of sleep. Each time I return to the night we first met, the night you made your debut inside my body, I remember your fervent request after our collective combustion.

'Spend the night with me,' you said.

I didn't, because even though I was younger then, I already knew the intimacy and danger implicit in the act. I wasn't worried about the repercussions the morning after—having to wake up conscious of the night's delirium, wondering if it was either a dream or a mistake, having to re-clothe oneself, take a shower, and be obliged to have breakfast together before going our separate ways. With you I wasn't wary of these formalities. I was more afraid I'd get attached.

Sleep has always reigned supreme in your hierarchy of indulgences. You've never understated your preference for sleep over sex. And in our first year together, in that long-distance phase, what you wanted most from me was that I spend the night with you, that I share your bed.

({})

We don't just sleep together, you and I, we perform the act of sleeping, we shapeshift through the night. When we begin, you are a wall and I'm this rich, green moss that's creeping over you, colonizing your surface. Midway through the act, I become an ocean wave. You caress me and try to surf upon my breadth until we are suddenly transformed into branches of two tall, fruit-bearing trees that, oddly enough, grow in each other's shade. Often we have to will ourselves to wake up, to shake sleep from our eyes, for we both know that given half a chance we could go on forever, shapeshifting like we are prone to do.

There's no approximate figure to encapsulate the number of conceivable sexual positions there are—the missionary, the cowgirl, the reverse spoon, the bend-over-backwards, the lotus, the standing position, the butterfly effect, the deep impact, the crushing spices, the swastika, the swing, the tortoise, the bicycle, the corkscrew and at least six thousand more. And yet, there's little written about the probable combinations and permutations of sleep patterns that two people can possibly share after the act of sex, or despite its omission.

You are fascinated by the subject of sleep. You love taking photographs of people in the throes of it. I asked you about this obsession once. You said you were curious about the superficial relationship between sleep and death; how, ostensibly, the two states resemble each other, as if death is merely a form of sleep characterized by the absence of a pulse. You reminded me of that biblical incident, when Christ is about to raise Lazarus from the dead: *Our friend Lazarus has fallen asleep; but I am going there to wake him up.*

You are well aware of the intimacy of sleeping with a lover. It far outweighs the primacy of sex. There are nights when our shared bed is a warm safe cove. Between the sheets you lie foetal-like, and I am attached to you by the umbilical cord that is my breath, and you feed off me as I nourish the texture of your dreams. And then there are nights when our bedroom resembles a war zone.

Over the years I have catalogued some of the forms we assume as we shape-shift through our sleep.

The Take-this-Waltz Position

This is how we begin our expedition. I'm usually in bed before you, but when you're about to emerge I shuffle with delight. You enter the bedroom. Your yawn precedes you. Then, with your back to me, you begin to strip off your clothes. I peep through the corners of the book I'm fake-reading as you unbutton your cotton shirt, roll off your trousers until you're left with just your socks and your underwear. You always take off your socks first, then for a few seconds you are completely naked. If it's summer, you wear a pair of shorts, if it's winter, a pair of pajamas and a T-shirt. There are aberrations, of course, sometimes you tire halfway and decide to sleep in your underwear, but I always beseech you to wear a shirt so your muscles don't get cramped by the incessant whir of the fan.

You slip into the bathroom, brush your teeth, take a leak, then head back towards the bed, turn off the lights, and enter. I feel for you in the fresh darkness. You lie flat on the bed. At first I was convinced you always sought out the right-hand portion of the bed (assuming you are facing the bed, left if you're lying in the centre). But you revealed later that your natural instinct is to occupy the side that's closest to the door. 'A symptom of claustrophobia' is how you referred to it.

So you lie flat and I move towards you. You stretch your right hand out like an invitation. I respond. I enter your embrace and angle myself such that the left side of my body rests against the bed while the rest of me is splayed over you. Your right hand oscillates between my shoulder blades and my lower spine. My lips are pressed against your neck, and while my left arm lies low against the bed, my right arm reaches out for your palm. Our legs are intertwined. In an aerial view we'd look as though we were waltzing.

The Teaspoon over Tablespoon

As you begin to cave in to the dictates of sleep, you shift positions. You turn your back to me and as you do, you draw my right hand over you as if it were a shawl. Then you enmesh your legs within mine and as you do, you stroke the length of my calves with your feet. My lips are now pressed against the nape of your neck, my breath resounds against your skin.

It is in this position that you let me assert dominance over you. Traditionally, spooning involves the close fit of the larger concave of tablespoon over teaspoon, the broader frame of a man's body over his female lover, hard flesh over wet mound. You force me into the role of sleep-watcher.

'Pull my hair,' you plead. I oblige. I guide you through your journey into the subterranean. I wait until the pace of your breath is relaxed, until I can hear the first tenor of a snore. Then I kiss you softly on your neck and forehead, draw the thin cotton sheet over you if it's summer, and turn away from you; we now assume our next phase.

The Still-Butterfly Effect

In which we both lie in foetal-like positions, but in opposite directions, so that the only point of contact is our asses. By now I've un-entangled my feet from yours, and eventually, our legs form a ninety-degree angle as do our torsos. We look like the letter 'X', but I like to think of this as the butterfly formation. From this point of stillness I begin my descent into sleep.

The 4 a.m. Intermission, a.k.a Separation Anxiety

Around 4 a.m., my eyes tend to open inadvertently; it has received the signal from my brain sent by my bladder. I unpeel the sheet, wake myself up, and head to the bathroom. By the time I open the door to return to bed, you've already woken up, having sensed my absence. I walk back into bed. I inch closer to you and around now we assume the hierarchic position. I press myself against you so that my face makes contact with your chest. Your head is angled such that the base of your chin touches the edge of my forehead. You wrap both legs over me, while your left arm sweeps over my frame. I am encased in you completely. If the earth had to cave in at 4 a.m., we'd die locked in this embrace. I think of the archaeologists from future generations who will excavate our remains. What they will deduce. Will they be amazed by how our individual bodies were trapped in different shelf lives? Will they see the poetry in the embrace, the peaceful succour of our bones? At 4 a.m. I often struggle with sleep. The warmth of your body is both soothing and arousing. I battle temptation. I resist the urge to steal into your naked body and arouse you from your slumber. Your heartbeat echoes against your rib cage and I can feel the light tremors. Yet, it is strangely paternal, how you hold me in this position. At 4 a.m., I let you become my protector, my saviour, my guide.

Variations

Before I proceed with any further documentation, I thought it best to intervene here and address the aberrations to this general narrative of sleep.

#1

For instance, on nights when you have angered me, when the unstoppable force that is your temper has reared its ugly face and you've said things you shouldn't have, delivered monologues without pausing to see how I'm collapsing under their weight ... On nights like these I do not occupy your bed. I lie on its margins. I put as much distance between us as I can muster, and I consistently turn away from you through the night. My pillow soaks in my tears, the soft breeze that floats in through the grilled window offers some solace. The tempestuous scene repeats in my head like a rerun. It seems familiar but each time I review it, a fresh flood of anger streams past my cheeks.

When you come to bed you perform the usual ritual with your clothes, then you enter and for a moment, hesitate. You see how far I've wandered from my usual location and you wonder whether to reach out or stay still. I know because I am attuned to your every movement. I have sensed the times you almost touched me in a gesture of apology, and the times you've tried to pacify me with ridiculous sounds, never a straightforward I'm sorry; always a pussyfooted move. Sometimes you feel righteous in your anger and do nothing at all, except lie on your side of the bed and fall peacefully into sleep while I lie sobbing on the deeper end of the shore. Hours later, when, with swollen eyes and thirsty lips, I've managed to finally surrender to the evasive arms of sleep, I wake up to find my body aflame with lust. As consciousness kicks in, I realize it's because you've besieged my body. Your left hand is wrapped tightly around my frame, your palm cupped under my right breast to contain me, while your left leg envelops what's left of me. Your insistent snoring confirms that this move of yours was unconsciously made, and despite being lost in the landscape of dreams, your cock is erect and it rubs itself against my cunt. You refuse to retreat from this position. I have no choice but to give up on sleep and stew in my juices.

#2

Of course, there are nights when you fail to make this compromising move. So I spend hours nursing my anger, shaping my resolve to leave you in the morning and never return. On such mornings I get out of bed early, brush my teeth and just as I'm about to exit the bedroom, you stir from your sleep and call out to me with a singular line, 'Come here...'

I do. I carry the weight of all my lost tears as I walk towards you. You pull me closer and you caress me with the guilt of a sinner begging for a sliver of forgiveness. I yield.

#3

There are nights when you count the hours to your departure. I hate your morning flights but you have this preference for reaching your destination while it is still daytime there. On such occasions the bed is populated with stacks of clothes and equipment. I'm usually exhausted from having to prepare your house for your absence since your apprehension about leaving me your keys persists despite my pleas to the contrary. But you're kind enough to clear my portion of the bed so I can sleep at will. Despite my best efforts I'm unable to sleep. My body waits for you to climb into bed and I always know when you do. But it's usually at some unearthly hour and though we go through our routine positions, you're already up by the time I wake up. In a few hours you are ready to depart. Reluctantly, I prepare myself to leave with you and say goodbye to your bed.

#4

Sometimes, after we've made it past stages one and two, and after I've finally managed to lose myself to sleep, I wake up to find the darkness vanquished by light. My eyes take time to adjust and when I finally come to, I find you standing on the floor furiously swinging a racket.

'Take that, you fucker,' you shout as you scratch the itch of a mosquito bite.

'How come they only bite you?' I ask as I grab the second racket and assume my position on the floor beside my end of the bed. We look comical, like we're playing a game of badminton with an imaginary shuttlecock.

We continue like this for about fifteen minutes, straining our eyes in search of these swiftly flying trespassers who have stolen your blood. You will not sleep until you've sought revenge. After you've electrocuted at least five or six of them, you beam with satisfaction.

'Let's go back to sleep,' you say.

And when we do, we start all over again from the first position.

#5

Every few weeks, the sciatic nerve that runs from your spine down the back of your right leg resembles a stone wall. You hadn't warned me about it initially. I discovered how painful it was for you one night when I woke up (just before the 4 a.m. indulgence) and found you crouched in your corner of the bed, your head supported by the adjacent cupboard, your right hand nursing the stubborn nerve. You wanted to sleep but the overarching pain foiled each attempt. I sat up and ran my fingers through your hair until you stirred.

'What happened? Why aren't you lying down?' I asked.

'It's less painful if I sit up.'

'Why are you in pain?'

'It's my sciatica. It's acting up again.'

'Why didn't you wake me up?'

'You were fast asleep. I didn't have the heart to.'

'Well, tell me what I can do.'

You lay on your belly. I sat beside you. You began to spew a list of instructions. I obeyed. I pressed my fingers against the surface area of the nerve and massaged your thighs. It was only slightly softer than stone. Then you asked me to position my elbow exactly over the center of your right buttock and nudge you gently. I followed your every word and within half an hour, the nerve had eased. You felt better and you drifted off to sleep.

By now you have learned to warn me when you first sense the impending ache. On nights like these I must fight my own drowsiness and patiently massage your thigh until the pain subsides and you can be eased into sleep. You have also suppressed your qualms about waking me up in case the nerve starts to tingle in the middle of the night.

#6

You told me once that you were convinced you didn't dream. I told you that we all dream, but not all of us can recall the contents of our dreams, however loose or lucid. I know you dream because I have sensed exactly when you've arrived at a nightmare. Your body gets tense, you quiver slightly and your lips let out small soft gasps. Instinctively I turn towards you and stroke your back until you ease out of whatever frightening landscape you're in and stumble back into less threatening worlds. Sometimes I wonder what torments you. You've lived through so much terror. You may not have been to war but you've photographed the half-eaten remains of riot victims, the devastation caused by cyclones and floods, you've seen human beings kill each other, and you've seen death even in those ostensibly alive. It frightens me to think of how damaged you must be by all that you have witnessed through your lens. As I circle the expanse of your back with the ball of my palm, I realize that I want to be your deliverance from bad dreams. I want to be the one who restores your faith in humanity, who guards you from the dangers of cynicism, who rescues you from your fate.

#7

Sometimes, right after the Teaspoon over Tablespoon Position I lie flat on the bed after I'm sure you're asleep, and I masturbate.

#8

What if I were to tell you that there are nights when I wake up feeling fucked, only to discover it was all a dream because your snoring is proof that you haven't at all stirred from your state of slumber. Each wet dream is vividly real and I can recall with precision the sensation of you having seduced me, of breathing in your body and having you sealed so fervently within my folds. I find it hard to believe I had imagined it all and while I'm disappointed to realize that the events in my wet dream didn't exactly unfold at all, I am thrilled by the exquisite rush that takes over me. I wake up wet and confused and surprised and elated and when I turn over to face you, I kiss your mouth. What I want to do is arouse you, but in deference for your preference for sleep, I choose not to disturb you. Instead I nurse my wet and aching cunt and I come.

You, however, have no inhibitions about acting on your wet dreams. I remember so clearly that one night, a year ago, when you shoved your hands inside my shorts and started to stroke me with a desperation you perhaps are only able to express while subconscious. I found I could no longer return to sleep. You had awakened my hunger. I stared out the window and watched the sky as it changed shades, lightening with each passing minute. And when the sun had made its appearance, I pressed myself against you and waited for you to harden. When you did, I proceeded to undo you. You seemed surprised by my move.

'It's all your fault,' I said to you as you moved inside me.

'Why, what did I do?' you whispered in my ear.

'You did unspeakable things in the middle of your sleep,' I said. 'You rubbed your hands against my cunt. Did you really think I . . .'

Just as I was about to complete my sentence, you announced your arrival with a loud, beseeching groan. Then you fell asleep over me as my fingers played with your hair.

#9

Some nights, when sleep is particularly evasive, I lie awake and listen to you snore. You told me once how you were afraid you were suffering from sleep apnea, but my intense study of your snoring patterns shows otherwise. There are no gaps of breathlessness between snores. In fact, I have deduced that your snoring condition is far from acute.

You're very polite about it. I've learned it's why you sleep on your left side, because you feel you snore less, and it's true, you do.

Your snore is phonetically composed of two syllables. Seldom do you snore in iambs, where the second syllable is stressed and not the first. Largely, your proclivity is towards the trochee, the first syllable is accented while the second is only slightly stressed. There are moments when your snoring builds up and you sound much like Coltrane at his fiercest. At other, non-musical moments, you sound like an out-of-tune trombone. On the rarest of occasions, you perform the ritual of silence. I call this the 4'33', your tribute to John Cage. For the record, there's been only one instance where your snoring was so loud and cumbersome, I had to wake you up and ask you to turn down the volume.

One night I felt inspired enough to record your snore on my phone's in-built Dictaphone. It's an eight-minute, nine-second long recording and it confirms the note I once made about how your snore is, on average, four seconds long, mostly all trochees.

#10

In my absence, I have learned that you do not bother with sleeping on your side. Instead, you sprawl over the length of the double bed and you colonize my pillow too so that your head rests against two layers of cotton stuffing.

In your absence, when I am doomed to sleep alone in my own bed in my home, I feel unhappy. When you are in town I grow so accustomed to spending almost every night in your bed that occasionally, when we've agreed to take a one-night break from each other, I find myself displaced. It is then that I realize how my body is now so habituated to our various positions that when 4 a.m. comes around, I wake up and am momentarily confused by the vacant space beside me. It takes a few seconds for my brain to compute that I am not in your bed.

The Twilight Position

Around 5 a.m. we retreat into our individual worlds of sleep. From then until we finally wake up, there is little contact between our bodies. I suppose these are the hours of pure, private, undiluted sleep, minus the melodrama, minus the erotica, minus the theatrics.

The End of Sleep

Based on my documentation, on average, there are two probable endings.

The first is the most likely. I'm nearest to the window and so I'm more prone to the poetry of sunlight kissing my eyes, stirring me from the dark world of dreams into the clear light of day. I turn towards you and I start to massage your back. There's a well-established pattern to my massage. I start by lightly pressing my palms against the surface of your back and eventually work up a vertical pattern wherein my knuckles travel across your spine and its neighbouring region with a consistency of rhythm and pressure. Then I sit up and I massage your feet. I begin by pressing the tips of your toes and eventually use the pads of my thumbs to make deep impressions along the length of your foot. I indulge you for a good half-hour until you finally decide it's time to get out of bed and begin the day.

The second is where you slip out of bed while I'm still asleep. I wake up and find you've disappeared and I've learned now it's because you've had your fill and can't have anymore. I'm still greedy, so I continue with my sleep. It took you some time but by now you've made your peace with it and no longer return to the bedroom to insist that I follow in your footsteps and wake myself up.

The Economy of Tears

I have never faked a tear.

Not for me the edifice of pretence. Not for me the artifice of suffering. Every salty drop my eyes have ever shed on your account or otherwise has been authentic.

I wish I knew the source of my flood. I wish I could tell you more about the origin of my tears, or how I devolve from a state of sobbing to a more uncontrollable state of weeping until I am momentarily emptied of all feeling.

All I know is, I shed two kinds of tears. One is more physiological. It is less salty and is not motivated by suffering. It is the consequence of bodily exhaustion. You've noticed it many times in bed, when I yawn incessantly and my eyes leak in response. It happens to me on mornings when you wake me up before I am ready to be woken. I yawn as much as I must have the night before and my face is similarly greeted with a soft stream of tears. This strand of tears also rises when I'm making small talk with onions as I work my way through the many petticoats that dress them, or when a speck of dust infiltrates my eyelids.

This type of shedding does not constitute crying.

You provoke the more insoluble variety of tears—bulbous,

crystalline, laden with the weight of emotion. These are the instruments through which I perform my act of crying.

It begins with a single tear that sits perched against the edge of a single eye, until it resigns itself to the gravitational pull of my angst. As the first tear meets its earth-bound fate, the next one starts to take shape until the gap between the falling of tears and the rising of new ones reduces sharply along with increased levels of humidity until I work up a more definitive pace. Sometimes I can hear them crash-land against a surface and it sounds like the breaking of raindrops. The deeper the grief, the more tangibly they fall past my cheek and create little monsoon puddles.

Although my eyes are ostensibly the source of this deluge, they do not feel the pain of this birthing of salt-water. The pangs run deeper. I have managed to trace them to a nerve that runs close to my heart.

When I was a child I cried about petty things. My tears were honest, but their cause insignificant in retrospect. Except for moments I cried out of fear, when I'd somehow manage to incite my father's temper. He never hit me with his bare hands, always used a cane, or a ruler, as a symbol, I suppose, to demonstrate that the need for discipline was at the heart of his reprimanding, that no malice was meant, it was strictly business, parental business. He would lash at either my palms or my legs. There was no standard prescription as to how many lashes one could merit. The beating usually lasted as long as his temper, as long as adrenaline coursed through his body. Sometimes when his fit had passed, he would hold me unapologetically. All I remember was the feeling of relief. When it was over I would continue crying, my body would continue in its state of shock for a few hours, and then all would be well again. Until the next time I'd inadvertently rouse his anger. I learned how to appease. I learned how to stare anger in the face. I learned to be patient. I learned to love my father despite his apparent cruelty. As I grew older, he gave up the cane and the ruler and learned to express his temper through language. We became equals. I learned to pacify him, to entreat him to see things through my perspective, to expose the pettiness of his tantrum through the tenderness of my words. I healed myself from the trauma of childhood. I was convinced my experience with abuse would make me stronger, more immune.

As I got to know you, as you began to expose yourself, I learned how wrong I was.

To say you are short-tempered would be an understatement. You are prone to sudden fits of rage when something suddenly clicks and shifts inside your brain and your mouth spews venom. You say things you know you don't mean, and then struggle afterwards to take them back. You try to keep yourself in check. You try to warn me about things that trigger your outbursts. I know, for instance, never to keep you waiting, never to yell at you or mock you in any way. But I cannot always control the impulse that leads to your anger. And, often enough, my feminism gets in the way. There are many moments when, try as I may, I cannot get myself to pander to your mood swings, so I meet your curtness with curtness and I pay the price in salt.

So when you break, when you deliver your turbulent monologues, I say nothing, I do nothing except cry, not willfully or consciously, but almost involuntarily. The act of crying is my complicated version of paralysis, an articulation of a state that lies between the two impulses of fight and flight. My gift of speech abandons me. Words swirl inside my head and form various permutations and combinations of sentences, but they are not transformed by the coherence offered by language. My mind replays over and over and over the scene that led to this state I'm in of heightened pain, adding, in the process, fresh salt to my wound.

You make a mockery of my tears. You are indifferent to my body's spill; in fact, you are frequently amazed and astounded by how you have reduced me to tears. You tell me that I should be stronger, that I should cultivate a resigned indifference to your tantrums, that I shouldn't let it affect me, that by crying I surrender my power.

You do not console me when I weep. You do not exactly know how to. You have led me to bouts of madness in every conceivable public place. I have wept, on your account, in all forms of transport—buses, autos, planes, trains, scooters, cars—and in all habitable spaces—stranger's bathrooms and living rooms, in kitchens and hallways, and corridors, on terraces and in basements. Every corner of this city has, at some point, speckled with deposits of salts from my dried-up tears. I have managed to stain clothes, books, sheets, pillows, plates, mugs, and everything in between, with the acidic fervour of my tears that bear, in each molecule, the memory of some fragment of pain you have inflicted on me.

The first time you led me down the underground of tears, you were as shocked by your influence as I was.

'So I guess the spell has broken. The veil has been lifted. You probably don't feel the same way about me.'

I should have read it for what it was—manipulation. I told myself that if I was convinced I was in love with you, I had to learn to love all of you, even the non-flattering bits. When I look back

I realize the slyness of your move—you were trying to challenge the intensity of my love for you by insinuating it was merely the consequence of a spell, a delusion, a blind spot. And with each subsequent act of cruelty you started to push the limits, stretch the boundaries to see how much I could withstand, to measure how long it would be until I cracked, until I gave up and abandoned you. You were trying to test the veracity of my feelings towards you.

It was a complicated game with lots of checks and balances. For instance, one evening, again, during our first year together, when we were still negotiating distance, when we lived in different cities, you went crazy on me about something as mundane as clothes. It was winter and I hadn't packed adequately. My shoes were shabby, as was my outfit. You wanted to make sure I'd be warm enough that evening. We were supposed to go to the opening of a show of your father's photography, and you were distressed by my apparent shabbiness. You wanted to remedy the situation, make suggestions, find alternatives. You started to nag, then badger, until you built up a little storm and I didn't know what to do. So I decided to flee. I opened the door and I ran away. You shut the door behind me.

When I got into an auto I received an SMS from you. It was curt but precise, and surprisingly free of grammatical errors.

'I don't think I want to see you again after tonight.'

That January evening, in the snare of a thick, foggy Delhi winter, I learned how hot a tear can be. As they strolled down my face, first leisurely, then like a torrent, I learned the significance of opposites—hot, explosive tears on cold, exposed skin.

I wasn't sure what to do. All my luggage was at your house, and you hadn't given me a spare key. So, after roaming the streets of Connaught Place, I decided to make my way to the gallery. I wasn't sure where else to go. I was the first visitor. I spent time with each photograph, fell in love with quite a few, especially the one your father took of you when you were two-feet tall. Your mother lay naked on a bed, a maternal smile on her face as you sat beside her and held on to her tits. As I stood there staring at the strange similarity between the way your infant fingers tugged at your mother's nipples and the way you tend to tug at mine, I heard your voice echoing against the white-cube space of the gallery. So I quickly walked over to a corner at the opposite end of the entrance. You left the gallery to speak to someone and when you entered, caught me staring at you. For a few seconds we simply made eye contact. Then you moved your right hand in the air, curled your fingers towards the inside of your palm so that only your pointer finger stuck out. Then you moved it back and forth to form a silent gesture. 'Come here' is what you seemed to say.

I obeyed, my heart still reeling from the impact of your message.

We stood at the threshold of the gallery. I wanted to tell you how I didn't care for clothes. That I had flown all the way just to be here for you, that I knew how important this show was for you, but I couldn't summon the words. All that emerged were a few tears.

You looked at me and you raised your right hand once more so that the flesh of your palm made soft contact with the surface of my left cheek. It wasn't a slap. It wasn't a pat. It was something softer and more vulnerable, something akin to love.

'Please don't run away on me again,' you said, and smiled pleadingly.

'I won't, I promise.'

'Have a glass of wine.'

'Sure.'

It has never been easy, but I've tried, relentlessly, to stick to my promise. I suppose what you wanted was that I stay, despite your badgering, so we could work things out instead of my running away from you. But there have been exceptions; there have been moments when it just didn't seem worth it to stay, and times when you didn't even have the courtesy to extend to me that choice.

For instance, one evening, during our second year together, when I had moved cities. You were disappointed because I'd been busy two nights in a row and couldn't see you because of that silly rule you had about my showing up at your door no later than 8 p.m. So I decided to drop in unannounced around 7 p.m. You opened the door, were surprised to see me. You let me in and then promptly went back to your desk. When I went up to you, expecting to make small talk, you blew your top.

'I have a million things to do. Don't assume you can just traipse in whenever you like. If you're free, and I'm free we can meet. If not, then let's just stay away. Please leave now.'

I walked out the door. You latched it from inside. I was too stunned to move; I sat outside on the second stair and wept. After a few minutes I heard the click of the inside door and before I could make a dash for the stairs you were standing in front of me.

'Don't worry, I'm leaving,' I said, almost reassuringly.

You said nothing. As I made my way down the lane near your house, I heard the roar of your Gypsy and before I could turn to look, you had whizzed past me and I lost sight of you.

I cannot remember how we reconciled, but clearly we did. And I think all was well until this other incident, when I was forced to renege on my promise and walk out on you.

It was more recently, sometime during our third year together.

We were scheduled to meet one evening, except your Gypsy had been given for servicing, and you were slated to attend an opening and then a private dinner in honour of an artist friend.

If only you'd left me your keys.

I decided I'd catch up with you at the opening and take the keys from you, then head to your house and wait for you to get back from the 'private' dinner to which you didn't want to take me.

Except, everything went off schedule. You'd already left the opening by the time I arrived. You went to the Press Club and hoped someone would drop me there, which of course, didn't happen, until finally, I had to meet you outside the venue for the dinner. Now that I was already there, you ushered me in and told me to stay.

And when we got home you unleashed on me a grand saga about how uncomfortable it made you, how you prefer to go to places alone and leave alone, that that was the way it has always been with you, that I didn't belong to your world and should stop trying to fit in or assert my presence in that hemisphere.

'You know what, I don't need this. I'm off.'

I was exasperated. I picked up my phone and my purse and I stormed out of your house.

As I walked out of your lane I suddenly remembered how much I had left behind. My laptop, my charger, clothes, books, cash ... So I walked back very self-righteously and rung the bell. You opened the door.

'Thank God you had the sense to come back,' you said.

'I haven't come back. I'm just here to collect the rest of my things.'

'It's really late. If you insist on leaving, can you just do it tomorrow morning? We can also talk then, after we've both cooled off.'

'Fine.'

That night we slept apart, all those unexplored continents reemerged on the atlas of your bed. I woke up early and collected all my things. I was about to shut off my laptop when it shut itself off. I panicked. I asked you to return to me my back-up drive that you'd borrowed. You did and even made the gesture of executing the back up. It meant I had to wait until you were done before I could leave.

You went back to your study to work. I waited until my precious files had been copied onto the external drive. When it was done I packed up my computer, picked up every tiny thing of mine that lay in every room, a pair of earrings, a set of bangles, a hairclip, a dupatta, anything that could be used to lure me back to you. Then I headed to your door and shouted, 'I'm off. Goodbye.'

'Wait … Come here.'

I stayed by the door of your study.

'What?'

'Can we talk?'

'What's there to talk about?'

'I'm sorry about last night. I didn't mean to get so upset. It's just that I'm used to being a certain way, and I felt uncomfortable having you around. I didn't mean to yell at you and I didn't want you to leave. But you have to understand that I've lived alone for so many years, I've become set in my ways, I've allowed myself to fit into the mould of a jerk. That's what I am, a jerk. And somehow with you I've managed to contain it to a certain extent. In fact, in my past relationships, I have been known to be physically violent.

I have a bad temper and I have some really horrible sides to me. But fortunately, you bring out my good sides. Also, I know that if I ever raise a hand on you, I'll lose you. I know that you will leave me for good. And I enjoy your company. And I have strong feelings for you ... So if you feel you'd like to stay, please stay, but if you want to leave, I want you to go in peace, I don't want you to have bad feelings or leave in a bad mood.'

I left.

I needed time to process all this information.

Later that evening I bumped into you at an opening. Your eyes lit up when you saw me. We drank many glasses of wine, smoked a lot of cigarettes, and when it was time to leave, since you were still Gypsy-less, you decided you would first drop me home in an auto and then head to your place. But when we got to the auto, you just told him to take us to your place.

'Just come home, it's easier that way.'

We held hands throughout the ten-kilometre ride. I closed my eyes through most of it and savoured the ecstasy of having your heart beating so ferociously close to mine, to have this current coursing through our bodies.

I rarely respond verbally to your assaults. Like I said, my body often just freezes into a paralytic state. All communication is limited then to the liquid upheaval that articulates itself on the canvas that is my face. I do not make eye contact. I lower my gaze and I try to will my fingers into stilling the storm by absorbing the tears.

You have, by now, learned to heed to Ovid's advice. You no longer let me carry my tears to bed. Instead, you have become more attuned to the rhythm of my unravelling. When I reach the pinnacle of my sobs, when words have abandoned me altogether, you come towards me and hold me in a stilling embrace that's fuelled by the violence of your passion. You come at me with the fervour of a blazing fire and then you hold me still in your arms and you kiss my neck as my tears spill over the cotton of your clothes.

Barthes has a revelation towards the end of his slim chapter in praise of tears in *A Lover's Discourse*. *I make myself cry in order to prove to myself that my grief is not an illusion: tears are signs, not expressions. By my tears I tell a story, I produce a myth of grief, and henceforth I adjust myself to it. I can live with it, because, by weeping, I can give myself an emphatic interlocutor who receives the 'truest' of messages, that of my body, not that of my speech: 'Words, what are they? One tear will say more than all of them.*

You have yet to learn how to appease my anger, just as I have yet to learn how to be more resilient in the face of your temper. For the moment all I want to hear from you in moments of such despair is a simple, effortless 'Don't Cry'.

Only Women Bleed

I've always bled on time. I hold you responsible for this sole inconsistency. You badgered me the whole day about random things that you ought to have let go of. By evening I was prepared to leave your house. I collected all my things—I had clearly failed in my endeavour to not populate your house with my belongings—and I kept them ready near your front door so I could make my exit the next morning. It was too late to leave then.

You saw me immersed in my gathering and asked what I was up to.

'I'm just collecting my stuff. You're leaving in two days. It's best to be prepared,' I said.

'You don't need to do this. All I was trying to tell you is you can't lead two lives. If you're staying here, be here, don't make random plans with your friends. If you do, then go back to your place, but if you're here, be here.'

'I'm just preparing for your departure,' I lied.

I had decided that I would spend the night on the divan. I didn't want to share your bed. It was past midnight. I was tired. I hadn't eaten enough all day. I was too distressed from all your nagging, I couldn't manage an appetite, though there was hunger, an aching hunger, and as you were yelling at me I felt faint, like I would collapse at any moment.

When I was done with my tantrum, I went to pee. When I had emptied my bladder, I tore off a few leaves of toilet paper so I could wipe myself. And that's when I noticed the crimson clot. I was perplexed. I was still three days due. I hadn't made preparations. I couldn't remember the last time I'd bled before my time. I pulled out a couple more leaves of toilet paper and rolled them into a makeshift tampon and stuck it inside me to dam the impending flood.

You had already moved into the bedroom by then, but I suspect you gathered I was in a fit. So you stood outside the bathroom door, knocked and said you'd prefer I come to bed so we could wake up early the next day. I opened the door and said, 'I'm sorry, I got my period. I wasn't due for another three days.'

'I don't care if you get your periods one week early or one week late. I just want you to come to bed now so we can have an early start tomorrow.'

So I did. I figured this was your way of reconciling with me. I followed you to the bedroom but I had apprehensions about reclining on the bed.

'I think I should sleep outside, I don't want to stain the bed.'

'Why don't you just wear some tissue inside so it collects the flow?'

'I already did that.'

'So then you'll be fine. It's your first day, it's not like it's the Grand Canyon that's about to go off.'

I think you meant to compare me to a volcano. Last I checked the Grand Canyon didn't explode.

'Fine,' I said, and occupied the fringe.

You turned on the air conditioning and, when it kicked in, you said, 'Isn't this better than trying to make a martyr of yourself by sleeping outside in the heat?'

'Yes. It's nice.'

In the morning you promised to go to the chemist to buy me a pack of sanitary napkins. Except, you were so immersed with your work, you kept asking for extra time.

'Can you hold on for another twenty minutes?'

'I suppose I could.'

But when I went to the loo I realized that the makeshift tampon I'd assembled just that morning was already soaked with blood.

So I found the number of a chemist who would deliver and arranged for supplies. I didn't have the energy to schlep downstairs myself, and as much as I knew you wanted to be useful, I somehow couldn't imagine a fifty-six-year-old you speaking across the counter, asking for a pack of Stayfree Ultrathins.

I lay flat on the bed until the delivery could be made. My back had started to give way. As I stared at the rotating blades of the fan, I thought about how this monthly spill has been the only constant in my adult life; this periodic shedding of tissue and blood, the agony of swollen teats and bloated flesh and all kinds of excess, this regular reminder that I was defying my maternal destiny.

When I was younger, what I feared most was staining the cotton of my school uniform. Now I dread the spasms along my spine, the stomach cramps, the retention of water that expands my waistline.

I'd taken to informing you each time I began the spill. I can't say why. Unlike men my age, you always seemed to understand.

You'd rub my back and the heat produced from the friction between your palm and my skin would soothe my nerves. You'd urge me to take a Paracetamol tablet. There's no point in needlessly suffering, you'd say.

That's what you'd done last night too; when you heard me moan in pain, you beseeched me to take something to soothe my nerves.

'I'm just so exhausted, I cannot imagine getting up again,' I said.

So you got up from the bed, consulted your medical kit and presented me with a painkiller and a bottle of water.

'Please take this,' you appealed.

I did.

'Is there anything I can do for you?' you asked.

'Could you rub my back?'

And you did.

It occurred to me as I was lying down that I may have been wrong about this being the sole inconsistency. There have been times, when you were away and when I was staying at my place with my two flatmates, when my menstrual cycle went for a toss. I remember researching it and reading somewhere that women in pre-modern times, with no access to artificial night light, ovulated with the full moon and menstruated in conjunction with the new moon. Even the word 'menstruation', I learned, shares an ancestry with the word 'moon'. Both are derived from the Latin 'mensis' which shares a relation with the Greek 'mene'—the root for the English words 'month' and 'moon'.

I remembered this one particular instance, when I was sure we would never see each other again. You were away in China, for some exhibition of your work. We'd had a terrible fight over the phone. You were bullying me about my not having finished this handbook. I'd taken a Midol for the first time during that especially pain-ridden period. It was supposed to guarantee relief. 'Anti-bloating, anti-cramping' were among the remedies it promised. It worked like a charm, except my bladder went on a spree and I watched as, each time, my blood spilled alongside urine. Inside me my heart was breaking, piece by precious piece, and it seemed as though the blood from the ache was flowing out from my uterus through my cervix into my vagina until it finally stained the manicured cotton of my sanitary napkin. In my mother's time they used white cotton cloth. Added to the pain of menstruation was the chore of washing off the stains, cleansing the cloth so it could be reused until it wore thin.

For those five days I wished I could have purged you from my system, the way I did my endometrium, flush you out of my being the way I did all the water I had retained, so I could then prepare my fertile womb for new seed, new yield, more promising possibilities.

As I waited for supplies, I wondered whether you had ever expected that at fifty-six you would have to contend with the vagaries of a menstruating twenty-six-year-old. If you were a woman you would probably have been either on the verge of menopause or on the other side of it. In all probability your womb would have to have been surgically removed. I wondered what it must feel like for you to even have to insist on a condom because I am young and fertile.

Sometimes I think about all our unborn children who've escaped through my womb because we couldn't risk seeding them, because you've grown too old for fatherhood, because you're too busy for the mechanics of it, too impatient and temperamental to be any good at it. My friends warned me that I may grow resentful of you for denying me the privilege of motherhood. The way I see it, I've chosen you over all my children. And if I resent anything, it's my womanly body that's constantly reminding me of the passage of time, that's holding me captive to primitive childbearing instincts, that refuses to stop ovulating and then bleeding, not until I arrive at the age you are now.

You've never been fazed by my monthly spillage. You've never let it come between us during the act of sex. In fact, I find it a bit bizarre how we tend to fuck more when I'm bleeding. From the first time we had sex up to the most recent instance. All you ask is for the extent of the flow so you can prepare by spreading a spare sheet that can absorb the leak. The last time we fucked the condom had turned red and as you drew it out of me where it had somehow got lodged, specks of blood spurted over and settled on you. I was afraid you'd be repulsed by it, but you weren't. You let me recover from the heights of our ecstasy and after enough time had lapsed, you went to the bathroom and brought back a bunch of tissues, then you wiped the stray pools of blood that had formed over parts of me. I walked to the bathroom door and left a crimson trail in my tracks.

'I feel like I just lost my virginity,' I said when I returned to bed. 'Like you broke me in.'

There was one time, just once, when you felt the condom slip. When we were done, you asked me casually how I was placed in my cycle. I was fourteen days in, at my most fertile. You said it was probably okay. For the next fourteen days I lived through the agony of anticipation. I oscillated between moments of hope when I wondered if perhaps your seed had taken root, and moments of despair when I knew it hadn't, that we had been safe. And on the twenty-eighth day, when I felt the first trickle, I mourned for the daughter we had unintentionally lost. It was a futile, hypocritical exercise because I know I felt relief that you hadn't impregnated my womb. I mourned not just for her, but for all the sons and daughters you and I may never have because our circumstances do not permit it.

'The womb is not a clock, nor a bell tolling,' Anne Sexton wrote in her poem 'Menstruation at Forty'. I know there is time enough for sowing and for reaping, for harvesting and for celebrating the spoils. What I don't know is whether I want to bear any fruit that doesn't grow from your seed. You have robbed me of my maternity but I do not resent you.

I have chosen you over posterity.

Housesitting Blues

The leak in your bathroom ceiling was an act of providence.

It was I who first detected it. I'd spent the day in your house and early evening I decided to take a shower. I entered your bedroom and as I took a few steps in, realized my feet were submerged in water. I called out to you and asked if you were somehow responsible for this. You seemed as surprised as I. I traced the source of the water to the wall adjoining the bathroom that faced the bed. Something had gone wrong because within seconds the wall was host to a waterfall. I rushed to the living room and grabbed a few sets of newspapers, which I then spread across the floor. I brought a dry cloth and a bucket and started to collect water so we could undo the mess. You rushed off to the neighbour's flat upstairs and managed to have the water supply turned off; it took at least half an hour before the spill could subside.

In three days you'd have to leave on an assignment. We were justifiably unsure of what the next move should be. Things were slowly falling apart. Stretches of the ceiling were threatening to dislodge themselves. The walls of what used to be your darkroom had turned damp too and we had to move all the things you'd stored there so you wouldn't lose them to the flood. It was a strenuous exercise for both of us.

One day before you were to leave, you told me casually that your downstairs neighbour was concerned about the situation. We got lucky this time because we were at home. Rather, I was at home with you. If you were alone, I'm certain you wouldn't have noticed the deluge until midnight, when you would have finally left your study to head to bed. But if the leakage were to resume in your absence, nothing could be done. We'd have to break down the door to get in. You'd have lost everything.

'Can I give you my keys while I'm gone?' you asked.

'Of course,' I said, trying hard to disguise my utter happiness at finally having possession of those few kilograms of metal I'd been lusting after for so long.

'Will you promise to call me should anything go wrong?'

'Absolutely.'

So you submitted your house to my care. You didn't exactly have a choice. You couldn't cancel your trip. It was the perfect solution.

Those seven days you were away were gruelling, to say the least. Each day a new calamity unfolded. One day it was the ceiling in the storage room, the next it was the geyser in the front bathroom that randomly began to squirt water at an enormous pressure.

And then there was the errant balcony drain.

One evening during that tiresome week, I went to an art opening. There was an installation that called itself 'The Panic Room'. It was meant to be interactive, so I stepped inside the square set of jute bags that lay on the floor and pressed the red button with my feet as instructed. The bags inflated around me and the square boundary transformed into a looming tower, entrapping me. All I could see beyond the four jute walls was a stretch of ceiling. I was unimpressed. I didn't feel any panic, in fact, I felt cocooned and calm and isolated from the pretentious faces that had surrounded me all evening. I sat down with my glass of wine. I was told to press the green button when I needed to deflate the walls, when I began to feel claustrophobic, which I learned later was the point of the installation. But I didn't feel ready yet to leave this jute shell. Suddenly, the jute bags began to deflate themselves, leaving me exposed. Apparently the panic room overheated itself because I didn't panic soon enough.

I went back to my place that night because I had a ride. I woke up to the sound of my phone ringing. It was your neighbour. She sounded distressed. She told me your balcony was leaking. I woke up instantly and told her I'd be over as soon as I could.

My breath started to collapse. My heart announced its fear and beat ferociously. The muscles around my chest started to quiver as I envisioned disaster. I retraced my steps. Yes, I'd definitely closed all the taps. I'd shut off the washing machine too, so this couldn't possibly be my fault. Why did this have to happen on my watch? It took you three years to trust me with your keys! I could sense impending doom. I should have slept in your bed last night. I shouldn't have abandoned your house for mine.

I ate my breakfast mechanically. I wouldn't have bothered but my flatmate had taken the trouble to whip eggs into an omelette and lace it with slices of Gouda. She'd even toasted bagels and had buttered them so they were ready to eat. I held the bread in my mouth and searched for the bits of Gouda but all I could taste was disaster. I tried to make conversation but every sentence was a dead-end that took me back to the subject of probable collapse.

Images flashed in my head at the speed of half-thoughts. As long as you were around we were partners in disaster. Still, I'd rather you let me house-sit than leave your home unsupervised.

I rushed over to your house and scanned the balcony from downstairs. Then I sprinted towards your door, negotiated the three locks that kept me from the scene of disaster. I headed to the balcony and felt confused. I couldn't find any water there except for the memory of it that was contained in the large stain in the corner beside the clogged drain. You returned my panic call and instructed me to simply unclog the drain. I did. I explained the situation. I told you it must have rained last night and since there was nowhere for the water to go, it seeped through the layers in the ground until it found four or five little outlets and then it began the process of catharsis.

I wished I was as calm and relaxed as I had been when the jute bags inflated around me in that artificially controlled panic room. I should have had more respect for the time zone you were in. I shouldn't have called you at that unearthly hour of morning and invaded your sleep. But nothing could have salved me. Your voice was the tonic I needed. 'Thank you,' you said over the phone and I knew you meant it. By then I had begun to leak salt water, little pearls had started to drip across my cheeks. I tried to say something in between my long, deep breaths but my malformed thoughts couldn't translate into sound. All I managed was a monosyllabic goodbye, after which you disconnected.

We know now that your upstairs neighbour was the one at fault. He had been renovating his house and quite obviously, your house had to bear the brunt of it. As a reward, though, you began to leave your house in my care more often than before. And even when you returned from your voyaging, you would let me keep one set of keys so I could 'be more independent'.

I relish staying in your house while you're away. I find the intensity of my yearning for you is less stifling when I sleep in the comfort of your bed. Although it takes me a while to fall asleep, I wake up rested, sunlight gleaming upon my face. I enjoy being able to maintain the same routine I'd have if you were here; making myself a pot of tea, opening the windows in the living room to let in the air and the sun, and spending the day working, the evening with a glass of single malt and writing my way into the night. The only glitch is my inability to eat alone. I hate having to cook for one, and while I don't mind eating alone elsewhere, I find it particularly difficult in your house. I've grown too accustomed to having you sit across from me, indulging me in conversation over dinner, drinks and cigarettes.

But everything was threatened a few weeks ago. You were out of town, I stayed back in your house. It was afternoon when you called to say you had reached Bombay. I told you it was unbearably hot. You told me to turn on the AC and park myself either in the bedroom or the office. I did as you said. Switched the relevant regulator on, turned on the AC and left the room to cool while I made myself some lunch, did a round of washing, put the clothes out to dry, and engaged in other household chores. When I was done I decided to take an air-conditioned nap. I woke up when I noticed the light flickering. I turned off the AC and went to the living room to work. An hour later I got a call from you. Your neighbours had called you to say they saw sparks in your front balcony. You asked me to take a look. I did. The wires between the two fans connected to the split ACs were on fire. It was a proper electrical fire.

The next half hour you recited a string of instructions, got me to turn off all the fuses so I could pour water to stop the fire, got me to check on random things to ensure there were no more sparks, and finally told me not to even think of turning on the ACs again. You said you'd arranged for someone to come home the next morning to inspect what had happened.

I agonized over it for hours. I knew I was not at fault. I'd done nothing wrong. But I was sure this meant the end of my relationship with your keys. This would be your excuse to take them back. And I was right. When you returned and witnessed the aftermath of the electrical fire, you knew we had got lucky. It could have been an outright disaster. The building could have burnt down. After you had the electrician fix it, you told me this was why you preferred to have the house locked. You could have lost everything, you said. I wanted to remind you of the times when my being in your house had saved you from ruin, but I thought it best to be quiet.

When you had to leave again, I kept all my things together so I could leave with you, like we used to do before. We woke up at six in the morning so you could pack. I made tea and then took care to ensure there was nothing edible in the fridge that would rot. I disposed of the leftover milk and curd, toasted the remaining bread, and packed the few tomatoes that were in the fridge so I could take them with me. I covered all the kitchen surfaces with cloth so they wouldn't gather dust, closed all the windows so the pigeons wouldn't colonize the house in your absence, and ensured everything was tidy and in place. You were still packing, so I lay down on the divan to catch a few minutes of sleep. When I woke up you were bathed and ready to go. I got up and rushed to get my clothes together so I could take a shower. But you stopped me mid-way, as you were wearing your socks.

'You don't look like you're ready to leave,' you said.

'No, just give me five minutes. I'll be ready. I'm sorry. I was just really tired and needed to sleep.'

'Listen, why don't you just relax. I'm ready to go, but you can stay and leave whenever you like. Keep the keys with you.'

'Are you sure?'

'Yes. Keep the keys but don't stay here at night because I'd rather you didn't turn on the AC. I don't want you to have to deal with fires and other calamities.'

'Okay.'

I helped you carry your luggage downstairs. The taxi was waiting. The same Sardar who normally drops you to the airport was ready to leave. I wondered if he wondered who I am, though by now he must have grown accustomed to seeing me with you. I kissed you goodbye.

'See you on the other side,' you said.

'I hope so,' I said.

You meant Paris. You were scheduled to be there in the second week of July. I was supposed to meet you there. It was the first time I'd come this close to actually making it abroad. There were just a few weeks left until my twenty-seventh birthday. I wanted to spend it with you. There was also the matter of my yet unfulfilled birthday wish made last year—to go travelling with you. The fate of my trip rested in the hands of anonymous visa officials. You did your best to ensure I could get this far. You badgered me into getting letters from relevant authorities and making all the necessary phone calls. I submitted my papers a few days ago. I was yet to hear back.

As clichéd as it sounds, all I wanted was to be able to look back at our romance years later, when we were probably no longer together, and remember with a tinge of nostalgia and delight that despite everything, we'd always have Paris.

'We'll Always Have Paris'

Travelling is an act of surrender. Language is reduced to sounds, some familiar, some absolutely alien. One is left at the mercy of strangers native to lands that had only previously existed in the cartography of one's imagination.

A virgin traveller, I played safe and chose France as my 'first' because the muscles of my tongue and ears still remembered the language despite having learned it almost a decade ago. And you were already there, so there was just the matter of boarding the flight, landing at CDG airport, ushering myself to the right platform that would escort me onto the TGV I'd booked to get me to Nimes, where I was scheduled to meet you at the bottom of the staircase at the station.

I saw your anxious body leaning against a shop front. You sensed my approach and turned to greet me. We grabbed a baguette stuffed with a delicious, generous serving of chorizo, and sat at the bus stop to board the bus to Arles.

These were the preliminaries of our first trip together on foreign soil, a trip that would take us through the photogenic streets of Arles, Nimes, Paris, Bergundy and Kassel in Germany, and then back to Paris.

I find myself unable to summarize the euphoria and the uncertainties I experienced during that fortnight together. I should have made notes. I should have carried a camera. I shouldn't have been so stubborn about using words to document what my eyes were seeing when a lens could easily have sufficed. But then again, I am no photographer, and who wants to see stodgy pictures that would simply have featured the two of us framed against a river, or a monument, or the countryside. What could they have possibly recorded that I would not have been able to recall in words?

For instance, I could have flashed a camera at that bum we encountered on the metro late at night when we were returning to the apartment of a friend of a friend where we were staying. His begging bowl resembled an ashtray, and he held it out at us almost arrogantly, like it was our duty to donate a cigarette or two, or some loose change. But instead of demanding our charity, he looked first at you and then at me. We were sitting with our hands interlocked, our feet so close to each other you could sense the circulating current.

'Lui, il est ton mari?' he looked at me and asked.

I understood him perfectly. You didn't.

'We don't speak French,' you replied, and in the breadth of a whisper asked me not to engage with him.

'Oui et non' is what I would have said, had you not appealed to me to be silent.

A photograph could not have captured the sagacity behind his question. Back home I'm usually asked if you're my father, it was refreshing to think that we could appear to someone as husband and wife.

Here, in the more tolerant French air, we found no need to

disguise our relationship. We walked the streets of Arles, Nimes and Paris like lovers in heat, drenched in the humidity of a previously undiscovered strain of intimacy. There were movements our bodies felt permitted to make that seemed unimaginable back home, gestures we wouldn't have dared to indulge in, in the suffocating conservatism of our homeland.

You and I have always worn a face to meet other faces. Our relationship never had a public persona. In the privacy of your home we could be lovers, but beyond the periphery of your door, the 'act' must begin, in which we perform the role of individuals who are unattached to each other. We never quite engaged in public displays of affection. It seemed inappropriate to do so, so bothered were we by moralistic eyes. Sure, we had our secret codes—a specific look to communicate attraction, or a teasing smile if one was ever chiding the other, messages relayed over the lifespan of a whisper. Our love always wore a clandestine gown each time we took it out for a stroll.

It was the Parisian air that seduced us. When we got in after journeying through the sunny towns of Arles and Nimes, it was still unusually chilly for July. It was a miracle we had made it this far given that by our third day in Arles, the insides of your body had begun to rebel, your stomach started to reject everything you devoured. I remember that night in Nimes when we walked from our hotel to the cathedral amid the wild wailing of an Argentinian Gypsy band whose music seemed to gush over the streets and seep into our very bones. We were on our way to the cathedral to hear a woman sing the '*Ave Maria*'. Mid-way, you asked if we could pause for a moment so you could sit down on a bench you had spotted. Your body was giving way again, that bilious feeling was returning, the nausea was settling in. We stayed still for a few minutes. You were beginning to surrender your body to my care. You tilted your head against mine, so it could find a resting place, however temporarily, and you closed your eyes as the gypsy music continued to ooze, drowning us in its invisible flood. We did make it to the cathedral, and we did hear the '*Ave Maria*', but fifteen minutes into the divinity of the experience, your stomach had begun to growl once more. You looked at me with half-appealing, half-apologetic eyes.

'I'm really sorry about this, but can we please leave. I don't feel very good.'

I smiled and held your hand and led you out from the cathedral back onto the streets, bought a few bottles of water for you before we returned to our hotel room. Soon after we arrived, you went into the loo and closed the door behind you. I could hear the unpleasant sounds of your body expelling the nausea. You returned to bed, lay down for a bit until you felt the irrepressible urge to puke once again. This time I followed you. I'm not sure why. It wasn't something I'd ever done before. Under normal circumstances you would never have wanted to let me see you like this. I went in on an impulse, and I held your head and I stroked your back while you attempted to banish the bile from your system.

'What joy, to have to re-taste food one has already consumed!' you said, and we broke into laughter, amused by the absurdity of the act of regurgitation.

You decided that night that you would temporarily stick to the softest of foods, like yoghurt, and water; a completely liquid diet minus any form of alcohol. And then, unnecessarily, you apologized once more for being sick. I stayed awake most of the night massaging your feet so I could ease you into sleep. When I was convinced you were safely tucked away in the land of dreams, I moved aside so I could also fade away. I cannot remember what hour of morning it was when I noticed you were up once again, puking into the commode, but neither of us could sleep after that. I was on high alert to make sure you were okay; you were too troubled by all the churnings inside your stomach to rest.

You felt better the next morning. At least you'd stopped vomiting. You were still weak, but you were adamant that we go sightseeing. So we did, and then got ready to leave around 4 p.m. to catch the train to Paris.

The fact of your mortality haunted us through the journey. Your stomach persistently rejected everything you devoured, although you tried to find ways around it; soft foods, easy-to-digest soups and juices, plenty of water, cut backs on cigarettes. You were almost okay the first few days in Paris, before we went off to Bergundy to see S.

When we arrived at X sur Argenteil, you seemed much better than before. We had a succulent home-cooked quiche and many glasses of rose. We returned to our room in S's beautiful thirteenth-century stone house, and decided to indulge in a siesta. I had just begun to menstruate, yet, I woke up refreshed, painkiller magic running through my system. You found the act of waking up too tiring to attempt. You drifted in and out of sleep, and by early evening, had begun to puke once again. I was on constant stand-by, holding your head up, stroking your back, and then massaging your feet when you returned to bed. S had already begun to cook the veal in white wine. She'd kept the *girolle* ready too. You urged me to keep her company, so I left you and went into her kitchen where she was opening a bottle of rose. I sat with S for at least an hour, enjoying each minute of our correspondence, savouring the warmth of her hospitality, the graciousness of her personality, and the fact that, unlike most of your friends, she took to me instantly. She's as possessive of you as your other female friends, but not once did she patronize me or judge the merit of our relationship, unlike M, who once told me to my face (in your absence, of course) that I was everything I was because of you!

When I returned to you an hour later with a cup of tisane, you had grown even weaker.

'Please stay with me for some time,' you appealed.

In that moment, in that candid utterance, something changed irrevocably between us. We had arrived at a new milestone. Where before, in moments of sickness, your impulse was always to push me away, to be alone, now you sought not just my company but also my caress, as if it were possibly a form of healing. You allowed yourself to reveal to me the side of you that is vulnerable and mortal, like you were drawing me into a secret place that no one else had ever been privy to, that even I was not permitted to enter until then. Thus far, I had only loved you in health, this was my opportunity to love and care for you in sickness.

It could have gone either way, the act of compassion. An associate, the wife of a renowned artist, who was in her early fifties when I made her acquaintance, told me, when I once asked her what it was like to be with someone thirty years older, that it was no different from being with someone closer in age.

'I have women friends who married men their age, and quite a few of their husbands had severe health problems, so they had to care for them much in the same way I've had to care for A,' she said.

However, their relationship changed dramatically when her husband had a serious heart attack when he was in his late seventies.

'It was then that he started perceiving me more as his nurse than his wife,' she explained.

When I came to you with a bowl of clear Miso soup, you were too weak to even sit up, but you mustered the courage. I held the bowl in my hand and scooped a spoonful to put into your mouth, but you wouldn't allow me this gesture.

'No, I'm not yet an invalid,' you argued.

'You're very sick, just let me feed you. Indulge me,' I said, after which you relented. But two spoonfuls later, you felt the urge to throw up once again. When you returned to the bed, you groaned.

'I feel like an old man on his death bed,' you said.

'Shall I press your feet?' I offered, hoping to pamper you.

'Can you just lie with me instead?'

So I lay beside you, your legs curled around mine, your arms engulfing mine furtively with all the might of your leftover strength.

As you faded into a form of almost sleep, I closed my eyes and listened to the echoes of your snores, and together, we drifted into a strange land that I had only ever dreamed of but had never encountered before, despite all my previous dalliances with romance. In our unsteady state of unconsciousness we wandered into unchartered territory and inadvertently stumbled into un-promised land, an unmapped space, which I, in retrospect, have decided to christen Intimacy. A surreal island space with no definite cartography where language is composed entirely of gestures, where words as we know them are redundant, where any form of verbal exchange, however profound or prolific, is irrelevant, where communication can only be facilitated through acts of seeming unmeaning. A private republic, where our two disparate bodies, each programmed by its own ordinary eternal machinery, have suddenly, in the aftermath of an unexpected epiphany, understood the triviality of one without the other. So that even the act of hurting becomes a manifestation of reluctant intimacy. We were now the sole inhabitants of a previously undiscovered territory, a land we had no choice but to carry back with us when we returned home, one that stuck to us so religiously we could no longer be what we were before. In that secret emotion, in that unstructured, ominous moment, we became eternal itinerants in the land of intimacy.

Was this why the bum on the metro looked at us the way he did? Scanned our knitted limbs, sized up our form, attempted to overhear all that our bodies were saying without even speaking? He gazed at us with the guilt of an intruder, as if he had caught us in the act of making love, as if we were under the false impression that we were the sole occupants of the train, like there weren't all these other bodies inhabiting the same space.

Until now we had always been lovers in exile, existing despite not having the comfort and security of either a designation or a destination. Now we had found a notional space, a conceptual territory in which our survival could be guaranteed. Refugees until now, we had finally found sanctuary.

Until I actually journeyed overseas, the question of why one travels at all remained a mystery. Why are we so inclined towards upsetting our settled domestic worlds in order to discover ones that we only heard existed, of which we knew so little about? Some say it is so that we can come back home, so that we realize that our destination was, in fact, to return to the point of our departure. *It is not necessarily at home that we best encounter our true selves,* writes Alain de Botton in his *Art of Travel. The furniture insists that we cannot change because it does not; the domestic setting keeps us tethered to the person we are in ordinary life but who may not be who we essentially are,* he continues. I had no intentions or illusions of travelling to France to find myself. All I wanted was to travel with you, to journey together, to experience first-hand the joy you derive from being elsewhere. So keen was I at the chance that we might finally, literally and metaphorically, always have Paris, I didn't fathom the extent of how indelible the experience would prove. When we returned, I understood that what I had taken back with me as a souvenir was the satisfaction of having arrived together, and yet, of having only just begun our travelling.

On the verge of my return, I tried to pack in as much as I could. A salad strainer, three little clay mugs I picked up from a flea market, five cloth pouches containing lavender, and copies of Anne Carson's *The Beauty of the Husband* and *Men in the Off Hours* that I'd bought at The Shakespeare and Company bookstore (which I was frankly quite disappointed by, I had expected a more intense inventory). My suitcase wouldn't clamp down, stuffed as it was with all the clothes I'd worn, all of which had imbibed the nostalgic scent of the Parisian air, and were lined with intangible, libidinous memories from all our many visits to museums and galleries. You would wrap one arm around my bust so that your fingers were perched precisely over one of my breasts. Then, while I was lost in a Caravaggio, you would lightly, almost incidentally stroke me until my body started to exude heat. If we were watching video art, you would sit on the bench while I sat on the floor with your arms placed around my shoulders and my head perched upon your crotch. The act of viewing art had never been as erotically charged.

Like that navy blue dress I'd worn on my birthday when, all day, I'd expected some kind of wildly romantic gesture. It was undoubtedly one of the best days of my life. And yet, on our way back in the metro, I accosted you about the absence of a gift. I realized later how it is so much in my passive-aggressive nature to expect too much on my birthday and set myself up for disappointment and resentment. You took great offence to my badgering, and finally hung your head down in some mixed version of despair and shame, and then, rattled by the look of disappointment that had colonized your face, I confessed that all I really wanted was for you to hold me and wish me 'Happy Birthday'. The next few stations rolled by as we settled into a wild embrace, red-wine induced tears streaming down my face. We walked out of the Félix Faure metro station and about fifty metres into our stride, collapsed into each other like a pair of long-lost lovers who had finally been reunited.

'Happy Birthday,' you said at the climax of our spontaneous embrace.

'I love you,' I replied.

'And I do too, more than I care to admit.'

That cotton dress, like the rest of my clothes, is adorned with these invisible imprints that sit upon the fabric like secrets.

In *Casablanca,* when Rick convinces Ilsa that she must leave with her husband Victor, despite the fact of their love, because he's 'no good at being noble', because it 'doesn't take much to see that the problems of three little people don't amount to a hill of beans in this crazy world', because if that plane leaves the ground and she's not with him, she'll regret it, maybe not today, maybe not tomorrow, but soon, and for the rest of her life, he uses an argument that has now been immortalized in film history. *We'll always have Paris. We didn't have, we, we lost it, until you came to Casablanca. We got it back last night.* He seeks solace in the persistence of memory, and hopes that she too may find succour in the act of remembering that brief historic time they spent together, years ago, that had sealed their fate as lovers.

The line is the equivalent of a souvenir, the kind that one picks up en route in the course of one's travels, one that is charged with emotional currency. Over time, this innocent souvenir assumes the equivalence of a charmed object, a talisman, one that we begin to rely on not so much to aid the process of remembering but to counter our human proclivity towards the act of forgetting.

That we must one day renounce our status as lovers is perhaps inevitable. The uncertainty of whether that will or will not come to pass is something we cannot control, despite our best intentions. If and when we part, there will be too many things I may have to surrender because they are so intrinsically linked to our affair. But Paris I will always retain.

Maps and Places to Visit

Botton, in *The Romantic Movement*, makes a compelling statement attesting to the multi-dimensional nature of the act of travelling. *Travel may more interestingly be read as a psychological rather than a geographic effort.* Given your appetite for cartography, for needing to compulsively know your location within the confines of a Google map, I'm not sure it's necessarily wise to dismiss the 'geographic effort' that travelling entails.

In my early twenties, I was self-diagnosed with cartographic dyslexia, a relentless incapacity to locate oneself on the latitudinal and longitudinal dictates of a map, a helpless incompetence with following directions, and an inability to mentally chart the contours of any geographical space visited or even inhabited.

You have never shown any sympathy for my topographical disorder. If anything, you have berated it, relegating it to being a symptom of a mere phobia, one that you are adamant I resolve.

Using a combination of memory, mnemonics and Google Maps, you navigated us through the streets of Arles, Nimes, and Paris. You were the conduit, and I was the willing follower. You led the way while I focused on losing myself in the imagery, the paraphernalia that made each of these cities so unique.

Mid-way through our French intercourse, we made a trip to Kassel, a German town on the Fulda River in northern Hesse, to visit the thirteenth edition of dOCUMENTA. After Kassel, we would return to Paris where you were to spend just two more days with me before heading to London for the opening of the group show you were part of. I was to be on my own for at least a week before I returned to Delhi.

It was when we arrived in Kassel and got off the Deutsche Bahn that I felt, for the first time, that I was indeed in a foreign land. France, though unfamiliar, never felt alien since I could speak the language, however brokenly, which meant I could converse with strangers, read restaurant menus, understand the signs and figure out announcements made in trains. Unlike you who can count from one to ten, I knew no German, never had the ear for it, and had never even accidentally learned a word or two. We got off the train and headed to the tourist office to pick up some maps and guides.

When we finally ventured into the city, I saw a tram for the first time in my life. We got on board and headed to the guesthouse we had booked. We dropped off our bags, freshened up, and headed out to get our passes and view the various installations.

The first night, after dinner, we headed to the tram stop so we could go home. We waited for a good ten minutes before we realized we should have been standing on the other side of the road. Of course, it was you who had the epiphany, and you decided to blame me for being inattentive. How it had become my fault was something I couldn't quite understand, so I asked you to explain. You saw my question as the perfect opportunity to lash out at me for never taking the initiative when it came to figuring out directions, or at charting our path, and for relying too much on you. One accusation led to another and not before long we found ourselves in the thick of an argument in which you threatened that from tomorrow onwards we would just part ways. All because I have difficulties reading a fucking map!

I managed to pacify you, but you laid down a condition, that I get us back home. You would silently follow as I struggled to navigate us through a city that felt persistently alien, the few Indians and Bangladeshis we'd met notwithstanding.

One hour later we were back at the guesthouse. My instinct had failed me multiple times and you finally had to step in and take charge. Safe in the warmth of fresh sheets, I collapsed into tears and accosted you for having put me on the spot, for having demanded too bloody much from me without having given me any time to mentally prepare myself.

'But how the fuck am I supposed to feel at ease when you're back in Paris and on your own when you can't even find your way around?' you demanded.

'Following a map isn't the only way to find a place,' I replied. 'I've always figured it out, asked people, read signs. I have my own methods.'

'I don't care. Tomorrow, you are going to navigate. I need to feel confident in your ability to find your way. I cannot be in London and spend half my energy wondering if you're okay.'

It was strangely comforting to realize that the source of all your anguish about my dyslexia stemmed from your own phobia about having to worry about me. It was a thought that sunk in while I was sleeping. When I woke up in the morning, I rushed to the shower so that when you went in to bathe, I could spread the map of the city and the tram network on the breakfast table and try, desperately, to acquaint myself with the landscape. I made elaborate notes, counted the number of stops on the tramline that separated us from our destination, and placed both maps in a separate pocket within my handbag so they were close at hand.

You were suitably impressed.

'See, you're not bad with maps, you just haven't tried hard enough.'

'Well, I can make an attempt if I prepare myself. What you did last night was horrible, though, and unforgiveable; you just put me on the spot. It's like what my father used to do when he was teaching me math. In the middle of dinner he would ask me "problem" questions and expect me to figure it out, and I would simply shut down. I have a morbid fear of numbers as a result.'

'You just have some irrational phobia about it. It's all so simple, you just have to figure exactly where you are in relation to the street you are on, then chart out whether you need to head north or south, or east or west, and then keep rotating the map according to the direction in which you're moving. Do the same thing with Google Maps, and as you're walking, keep memorizing landmarks; that way you can always find your way back.'

({})

If only memories could be mapped. If only they could be given shape and contour, definition. The other day when we were recounting our experience at Kassel to R, who had also visited, I mentioned the fact of our fight about my dyslexia and how you had given me the toughest time. What amazed me was that you had no recollection of the subject of my retelling, as if it had never happened.

Anne Carson, in *The Beauty of the Husband*, her exceptional treatise on the death of a complicated relationship and the unsuspected awakening into beauty, has a stellar all-caps, run-on sentence-long section title—*DO YOU SEE IT AS A ROOM OR A SPONGE OR A CARELESS SLEEVE WIPING OUT HALF THE BLACKBOARD BY MISTAKE OR A BURGUNDY MARK STAMPED ON THE BOTTLES OF OUR MINDS WHAT IS THE NATURE OF THE DANCE CALLED MEMORY*. This ambiguous tease of a title is steeped in metaphors about the transient, unreliable, imaginative nature of memory, the tendency towards erasures and rewriting, its similarity to the process of selectively staining or imprinting events onto our minds such that the details slip out, like why or when the stain came to be.

Sometimes I have no sympathy for your amnesia. It is as though you have some kind of phobia about remembering things that are most phenomenal; moments we have shared that have possibly altered the course of our being. It is as though I see memory as a room or a sponge, while for you it is a careless sleeve wiping out half the blackboard by mistake, and it makes me wonder what will remain, if anything at all will, after the dance is over.

How will you navigate through the lifelines of this discourse between us with no Google Maps to lead the way?

How must I reconstruct all the spaces we unravelled, all the distances we travelled with our wanderlusting feet? How do I recover those moments and pin them down, make a map of collected memories?

Or is it at all possible that in the end, what will matter most is not what we will have remembered but all that we forgot? All the details that slipped so silently into eternity, all that vanished before we could understand, all that we can never recover first-hand, in word or thought or deed, all that passed before we learned to read with our ears and listen with our skin, all that was never spoken, all that we let in but never heard, could not feel, all that we left undone, unanswered still?

We are all that we have lost.

We are all that we are yet to lose.

Displacement

I returned from Paris towards the end of July. Instead of going directly to my house to deposit my suitcase, you invited me to come to you. I landed around twilight. My baggage, however, would arrive the next day. Air France had messed up.

A week later my landlord gave me and my flatmates an informal eviction notice, which meant I had to go through the tiresome drill of having to scour the city for a reasonably priced place to live. I had to give up the arrangement I had with the two other women I lived with. We had all agreed it was time to move on with our lives and part ways. S was keen to live alone so she could have her boyfriend over whenever she liked. M's budget was too restrictive. I was tired of living like I was still in hostel. This would be the third time I'd have to move since I made Delhi home. I was enthused by the thought of new possibilities but fettered by the uncertainty that came along with it. I found myself spending more time at your house, in denial of my situation, wishing that your apartment could be a more permanent home. Until one morning, while on my way to the market, I stumbled upon an idea: couldn't I just move closer to you?

I was increasingly annoyed by that seven-kilometre schlep

that separated me from you. Autorickshaw fares were on the rise. Besides, the whole affair was just an inconvenience for me; my clothes, my belongings always stashed away in a room I was paying for but barely living in.

I told you about my epiphany. You were sceptical. You discouraged me, told me I was sure to find cheaper houses about two kilometres away. But I was adamant. I had already imagined the convenience of it. Despite your advice, I went and spoke to a realtor and made an appointment.

I fell in love with the second apartment I was shown. It was on the second floor of a building located on the corner of a street that was separated from your street by 200 metres. No structural interruptions for at least 180 degrees, which meant that throughout the course of the day, sunlight streams through like a constant revelation.

The day after I moved in, I calculated the distance between your house and mine. Three minutes-long. The length of a song.

What We Talk About When We Talk About Love

Post midnight.

We stumble through the door. I reach into the kitchen for a draught of water. I bring you a glass. Red wine is dancing within the recesses of your circulatory system. You always drink more hastily than I, so I am always mildly inebriated while you veer towards intoxication.

I return the glass to the kitchen counter. I place an empty bottle under the RO filter. I cap it when it's full and take it to the bedroom, along with my phone, both of which I place beside my side of the bed.

I move towards the sofa and begin to unfurl my sari. I unhook my blouse and place both items of clothing in an untidy pile. I reach into your cupboard and pull out a T-shirt. After having clothed myself, I walk into the bathroom, lean over the sink, remove the bindi from my forehead and place it on the mirror frame, in company with the other bindis from previous occasions. I wash and dry my face, and then I lie on your bed and draw the sheet over me.

Three months into the New Year and it seems as though winter has renewed its lease. The nights are distinctly chilly when they ought to be balmy. Which means there is no need for the respite offered by a whirring fan.

I pick up my phone and look for the Shortyz app. I pull out the LA Times Crossword and start to decode the clues while anticipating your arrival.

Half-way into my crossword, you enter the bedroom, shut the door behind you, undress, put on your night clothes, move towards the bathroom, brush your teeth, return towards the bed, turn off the lights, and crawl in.

I turn off my phone and place it near the water bottle. I move towards you. I have to make an effort since you've veered closer towards the edge of your corner. Foreseeing your accusation the next morning implying it was I who cornered you, relegating you to a small fraction of the surface area of the bed, I urge you to move closer to the centre. In fact, playfully, I physically move you closer to what I consider to be the bridge[3] between our individual sides;

---

[3] Intriguingly, in Ali Smith's *Artful*, an insightful, genre-bending book about a narrator who is haunted by the ghost of her former lover, who, around the time of his death, was writing a series of lectures about art and literature which the narrator decides to complete in his absence, there's a passage towards the end of Chapter 3, 'On Edge', when an uncanny imagining on her part has suddenly been decoded, the narrator is mystified. It is nighttime and she decides to hit the sack: 'I got in on my side and put my head back on to the pillow. I stretched an arm and a leg over to your side of the bed. Then I moved my whole self to the middle of the mattress, actually the best place in the bed for a good night's sleep.' I would have included this passage in my treatise on our sleep patterns, but I chanced upon *Artful* much later and was amazed at the significance of that one phrase: the middle of the mattress. It is interesting that when either of us sleep alone in bed, like when we take our afternoon siestas, we both tend to occupy the centre, as if it were indeed a bridge connecting us to the absent

I tug at your hips with my fingers, compelling you to move closer.

Playful laughter.

'I don't want you accosting me tomorrow.'

'For what?'

'For pushing you to the corner.'

'Now kiss me,' I say.

'Why?'

'Because ... Because you love me.'

'How can you assume that?' you ask.

'What do you mean?'

'That I love you? How can you just assume?

'Really?'

'After five ... well, almost six years of our being together, you're still not convinced you love me?'

'I may. Or may not. But how can you just assume I do?'

'It's not an assumption. It's based on facts. You yourself have said that you do ... that you love me. About four or five times since we met. To my face.'

'How long ago was the last time?' you ask.

'Um. Maybe in July? In Paris? Or maybe last October? In any case, saying you do or not saying you do ... it doesn't mean anything. I used to be with someone who told me everyday for six years that he loved me, and when push came to shove, I realized that he didn't after all ... And, hello, you're the one who pursued me in the first place!'

---

other. As if in the act of occupying it, we could suddenly, magically, be two people at once. It is not as though our identities merge, but it is as though they exist on the edge of each other's consciousness. Sleep with the absent present.

'Oh really?'

'Yes, you're the one who urged me to come to Delhi,' I remind you.

'What was the context?'

'What do you mean?'

'Well, I don't see why my telling you to come was important in any way. You came here to work.'

You entwine your legs with mine and draw me closer to you.

'I'm not talking about the time I moved to Delhi. I'm talking about the first time I came to see you in Delhi,' I say.

Long strokes along the length of my back.

'When was that?'

'August 2008? Just a few days after we met. We met on the 2nd.'

Strokes continue. I start to melt.

'You're a pretty girl. I'm sure I would have told anyone in your place to come to Delhi.'

You do a mock imitation of a Casanova-like character.

'Oh. I see. I thought I was—'

'Special?'

'No. Different.'

Your fingers move along the surface of my thighs. So close—

'Wow. That changes everything. I was reading it all wrong. So you don't love me!'

'That's not what I'm saying.'

'What are you saying?'

'It's not that I'm not certain. I just can't commit to it the way you do. Are you going to start crying and get all hysterical?'

'No. I'm not. Or I don't intend to. I am crying. But that's because I feel—'

'Hurt?'

'Betrayed. I don't understand. What are you afraid of? I mean, it's not like if you were to declare it, I would beg you to marry me, or have me move in with you. We both know that isn't going to happen.'

'But you are secretly looking for some kind of commitment, aren't you?'

'How can I possibly ask you to commit to me when I am not sure myself about whether I want to commit to you or not, or if I'm even able to in the first place?'

'That's good to know.'

'So why are you with me then?' I ask.

'What do you mean?'

'It will soon be six years since we met. Why continue this? Why am I here in your bed?'

'Can you pull my hair?' you ask.

'Sure.'

I lean towards you and toss my right leg over your legs and draw you closer to my cunt. I run the fingers of my left hand over your hair and start to pull at small bunches. I can hear you purr under your breath. My lips crouch against your neck.

'There are different levels to it,' you say.

'To what?'

'To us.'

'Okay.'

'On one level there is the warmth and comfort I feel when I'm around you. You have this feminine touch. Then there's the intellectual connect. We understand each other. I can talk to you about things and you understand. Then there's our work relationship. We work well together. You help me out with my work. Then there's this emotional connection. I care about you very deeply. I have very strong feelings for you. You bring out my good side. No one else has done that before. And then there's the attraction. I am very attracted to you. The thing is ... I just feel that with something like love, it is easier to show it than to talk about it.'

'That's what I was saying.'

'I may find it difficult to say it to you. But suppose something were to happen to you, I would be the first person, I would go out of my way to be there for you. I know I don't do, or haven't done, as much for you as you have for me. But if you were ever in a situation where everyone else abandoned you, I would still be there. I would fight for you.'

Pause.

'This is all I want,' I assert.

'And what is *this*?'

'Home. I want to be home.'

'And where is home?' you ask.

'This. You. Us. This is home. This is what I want.'

As we kiss you confront the wetness of my cheeks and the salt of my tears.

'Listen. Don't get emotional. Don't take what I'm saying seriously. I'm drunk. I'm just babbling. This is all just a babble. I'm not declaring anything. I'm just babbling.'

'So you don't mean anything you're saying?'

'No ... I mean I'm babbling. I've no control over what I'm saying. So don't be waking up tomorrow morning complaining that I offended you.'

'Okay.'

'Anyway, this is the kind of conversation we should have when I'm sober,' you say.

'But we seldom do ...'

'Anyway. Listen, in the end everything is maya. Everything is impermanence. We don't really even exist. This thing between us doesn't really exist either. It's all maya. If there's one Hindu principle I subscribe to, it's maya.'

Seconds later, you nod off to sleep. I kiss you, turn sides so that my back is now against yours, and I masturbate.

({})

Barthes, in *A Lover's Discourse*, refers to the utterance of the words 'I Love You' as 'The Love Cry'. *Once the first avowal has been made, 'I love you' has no meaning whatever, it merely repeats in an enigmatic code—so blank does it appear—the old message (which may not have been transmitted in these words). I repeat it exclusive of any pertinence, it comes out of the language, it divagates—where?* he writes.

Barthes seems to suggest that this love cry is a feverish symptom of the pathological condition of being in love, an unavoidable consequence, an inevitable utterance with all the pathos of a desperate shriek, one that may or may not find resonance with the object of the lover's desire. It is as though, at the moment of its utterance, language loses its significance and connotes nothing except a longing for the loved one to empathize with the disease that has led to this repeated announcement.

To love, according to Barthes, is a *socially irresponsible word* which doesn't even exist in the infinitive except by a *meta linguistic artifice*, and the continued avowal of this state of being in love is one without nuance, one that suppresses explanations, an exorbitant paradox of language. *To say I love you is to proceed as if there were no theatre of speech,* he writes, which relegates it to the level of performance. It is: *Not a sentence. It does not transmit a meaning, but fastens onto a limit situation, the one where the subject is suspended in a specular relation to the other.* According to him, to try to write love is to confront the muck of language; *that region of hysteria where language is both too much and too little, excessive.*

({})

Mid-way through *Essays in Love,* Alain de Botton's narrator finds himself in a quandary. It is his girlfriend Chloe's birthday, and despite his contentment over the gift he bought her, the red cashmere pullover that she'd been dropping hints about wanting, he realizes, while wrapping his present and writing out a card that he had still not told her he loves her, despite being aware that he did. *Pullovers may be a sign of love between a man and a woman, but we had yet to translate our feelings into language,* he says. *It was as though the core of our relationship, configured around the word love, was somehow unmentionable, either too evident or too significant to be uttered.*

The narrator, in the course of the essay titled 'Speaking Love', comes close to Barthes' proposition, that to write love is to confront the muck of language. He compares love to a species of rare, coloured butterfly, *often sighted but never conclusively identified.* The other problem in declaring love, according to him, is that the very language of love has been corrupted by overuse.

Words like love or devotion or infatuation were exhausted by the weight of successive love stories, by the layers imposed on them through the uses of others. At the moment when I most wanted language to be original, personal, and completely private, I came up against the irrevocably public nature of emotional communication.

Finally, when he was on the brink of articulating his love cry in the stereotypical mode, he spots a plate of complimentary marshmallows near Chloe's elbow and has an epiphany. *It suddenly seemed clear that I didn't love Chloe so much as marshmallow her. What is it about a marshmallow that should suddenly have accorded so perfectly with my feelings towards her I will never know, but the word seemed to capture the essence of my amorous state with an accuracy that the word love, weary with overuse, simply could not aspire to. Even more inexplicably, when I took Chloe's hand and told her that I had something very important to tell her, that I marshmallowed her, she seemed to understand perfectly, answering it was the sweetest thing anyone had ever told her.* From then on, for the couple, the word love became distinguished and personal. *It was a sugary, puffy object a few milimetres in diameter that melts deliciously in the mouth.*

({})

My favourite poem by Kamala Das is 'In Love', from her collection, *Summer in Calcutta.* With each successive reading of this poem over the many years I have been in love with you, the last six lines increased in resonance. The poem, set in summer's heat, in the 'burning mouth of sun, burning in today's sky' mirroring her insatiable thirst for her anonymous lover, speaks of the meaninglessness of the utterance of the love cry.

Where is room, excuse or even
Need for love, for, isn't each
Embrace a complete thing a finished
Jigsaw, when mouth on mouth, I lie,
Ignoring my poor moody mind
While pleasure, with deliberate gaiety
Trumpets harshly into the silence of
The room ...

She brings the poem to its exhilarating climax as she speaks about the moonless nights ...

... while I walk
The verandah sleepless, a
Million questions awake in
Me, and all about him, and
This skin-communicated
Thing that I dare not yet in
His presence call our love.

There is an element of fear and uncertainty she feels even at the thought of making public the intensity of the passion between her and her lover. The words 'dare not' imply a kind of self-imposed directive, a prohibition, and, followed by the chronologically bound 'yet', they suggest that the time has not yet arrived for any such affirmation of love. There is even a trace of a threat, as if to admit to such an intense emotion would be to sabotage the affair. I love that she refers to the lover's 'presence', rendering it with philosophical implications such that it isn't limited to the fact of his being present, but the aura of his presence, as though it is for her a gateway into a private world that is only tangentially attached to the solar system by the existence of the melting sun.

There is a suggestion that perhaps, in due course, she may make an avowal, but now is not the time. For the moment, his mouth on hers is substance enough. I also enjoy the hint of presumption in the last line. She doesn't hesitate in believing that the skin-communicated thing between her and her lover goes both ways. All the fear she may feel in 'not yet daring' gets undercut with the mention of 'our love'. There seems to be some kind of implicit understanding on the part of both lovers as to what this 'love' embodies and the mystery of it makes it distinctive.

Das, rather craftily, confronts the muck of language and writes love, but not by any immediate avowal, rather, through *differance*, by underscoring the non-verbal dialogue between lovers that occurs sensually, where the skin is the receptor and the communicant, and verbal language is best delayed, and by privileging the written almost-avowal or the promise of avowal over the spoken love cry, and by connoting what their love is not by implying what it currently is, while simultaneously proposing, through her use of the word 'yet' that the future can negatively or positively destabilize her present notion of what their love signifies.

({})

Speaking of differance, I am tempted to reference this YouTube video in which an interviewer, Amy, asks Derrida, the profound literary theorist, if he could say something about love. The grey-haired, though rather handsome-looking Derrida tries hard to conceal his sense of amazement at the ambiguity of the question. His voice betrays him, though, and he sounds unmistakably annoyed by the myopic expansiveness of the question, which in the original French, was, 'Ce que vous desirez dire de l'amour'? His first response is confusion, followed by a witty rejoinder, a *jeu de mots* that serves as an excellent testimony to his entire treatise on difference. He says, 'L'amour or Le Mort?' (Love or Death), which, when he enunciates in French, sound alarmingly similar phonetically. The interviewer, whose first language is definitely not French, emphasizes she meant l'amour, pas le mort. 'We've heard enough about death,' she adds. 'L'amour?' Derrida asks once again, just to be sure. 'L'amour,' she reaffirms. And as he replies, you can see his lips contorting into a slight grin, a consequence of his surprise. 'I have nothing to say about love,' he replies assertively in his native French. 'Nothing ...' he continues somewhat irritably. 'At least pose a question. I can't examine "love" just like that,' he adds, bringing me back to Barthes' hypothesis that to write love is to confront the muck of language, that region of hysteria where language is both too much and too little, excessive.

'You need to pose a question. I'm not capable of talking in generalities about love. I'm not capable. Maybe that's what you want me to say in front of the camera,' and as he says so, he looks sideways into the lens and laughs. The interviewer now has no option but to actually pose something resembling a legitimate question. 'Could you explain why this topic has concerned philosophers for centuries? It's an important philosophical subject, isn't it?'

But Derrida is not to be placated. 'You can't ask this of me, Amy,' he says, and then repeats the question so he can hear it aloud once more and comprehend its explosive vastness. Finally, he seems to launch into an answer. 'That's how philosophy started,' he says, but again he stops himself short. 'No, no. It's not possible.' His next statement seems to be made after a lapse, you can tell that there was a cut, a break in the narrative, that the film's editor left something out. The next frame shows a more apologetic Derrida. 'I have an empty head on love in general. And as for the reason philosophy has often spoken of love, I either have nothing to say or I'd just be reciting clichés.'

So Amy has to rephrase her question once more, she has to be more specific. She attempts another round, but her question remains as vague, like she has no real gist of the main arguments made around the subject of love within philosophy. When in doubt, quote Plato, and that's exactly what she does. 'Plato often spoke of this, maybe you could just talk about that?'

By now somewhat irate, Derrida decides to interview himself. 'One of the first questions you could pose ... I'm just searching a bit ... is the question of the difference between the who and the what. Is love the love of someone or the love of something? Okay, supposing I loved someone, do I love someone for the absolute singularity of who they are? I love you because you are you (he points his finger towards the camera). Or do I love your qualities, your beauty, your intelligence? Does one love someone, or does one love something about someone? The difference between the who and the what at the heart of love, separates the heart. It is often said that love is the movement of the heart. Does the heart move because I love someone who is an absolute singularity or because I love the way that someone is? Often, love starts with some kind of seduction. One is attracted because the other is like this or like that. Inversely, love is disappointed and dies when one comes to realize the other person doesn't merit our love. The other person isn't like this or that. So at the death of love, it appears that one stops loving another not because of who they are but because they are such and such. That is to say, the history of love, the heart of love, is divided between the who and the what. The question of being, to return to philosophy—because the first question of philosophy is What is it "to be"? What is being? The question of being is itself always already divided between who and what. Is "being" someone or something? I speak of it abstractly, but I think that whoever starts to love, is in love, or stops loving, is caught between the division of the who and the what. One wants to be true to someone—singularly, irreplaceably—and one perceives that this someone isn't x or y. They didn't have the qualities, properties, the images that I thought I'd loved. So fidelity is threatened by the difference between the who and the what.'

({})

I was still dying when I met you. I just didn't know it at the time. I wasn't wise enough to recognize the symptoms. I couldn't fathom that the cancerous numbness that had besieged my heart was in fact the consequence of multiple stabs being consistently delivered at the hands of a scorned lover. I was barely seventeen when I first met him. I was so pitifully young, nubile and naïve. He, four years older than I, an economist and armchair philosopher, had aroused my appetite for the intellectual. He found in me facets that I always wished existed; beauty, intelligence, vivacity. He had a flair for language, a penchant towards rationality, and a tendency towards self-pity. Our initial correspondence was entirely over email, which nourished my hunger for wordplay, and within a week of consistent dialogue, I knew I was in love with him. It took him longer to gauge the depth of his feelings for me. You see, he had just died before he met me. He had been burnt at the hands of a woman who had fallen in and out of love with him before he had the time to even experience limerence. At twenty-one, when I first moved to Delhi, it was to live with him. He had relocated his life from Bombay and had started work with a public policy think-tank. We lived in a less than modest barsati in Green Park, for a full year, until he shifted to Hyderabad to advance his career. That was the second betrayal among many subtle ones that were to follow. The first remains too painful to recount.

A staunch libertarian, he had envisaged our relationship as a utopic experiment. 'Your body is yours,' he would tell me. 'You can be with whoever you want, just don't tell me about it.' At twenty-two, with him away in Hyderabad, with my having set up residence in that tiny quarter in JNU that was allotted to me, tasting, for the first time in my life what it meant to be independent, and sampling, almost virginally, the alluring world of desire, I drank in everything that came my way, I drank so much, so quickly, and so thirstily, that I soon grew intoxicated by the pleasures of pursuit. No more was I the insecure, coy, small-town girl who was oblivious to her own charms. I tumbled dizzily into the world of heat and lust, the land of fuck. I inscribed every man I conquered in the pages of my notebook, and soon, my writing was drenched in the exquisite wetness of desire. The lover remained a constant, I never doubted my feelings for him, but I was able to separate, with calculating precision, the universe of love and the paradise of sex. I had a pattern: I often chose men who were either wanderers or settlers on the verge of departure. I sought men who had no strings to attach, who appreciated the virtue of intellectual foreplay, men who had a peculiar talent for persuasion, men, who, when they finally had you pinned against them, made you wonder if you had been seduced or if this was what you had wanted all along. I revelled in this newfound ecstasy, and each orgasm brought me closer to the world of words. I came against my private landscape of thoughts, it wasn't blood that would rush to every corner of my brain but whole sentences, syllables gushing through my circulatory system, language seeping through my pores, each sigh a turn of phrase dying to be archived.

Until one morning, after a stretch of sleepless nights spent making love to J (the sleep-fucker), days before I was to leave university and return home, I found myself besotted by him. Soon it was mid-May, the season of returnings. I was back in Bombay, had spent my last hours in Delhi with J so that I had barely any time to pack my things and I had to leave so much behind. J was back in Paris, but before leaving, came to visit me in Bombay and we spent three nights together on the kitchen floor of a friend's apartment. G was done with his stint in Hyderabad and was back in Bombay. He'd been accepted into Columbia and there were barely three months to go until he left for New York.

J had seeped into my body and the scent of him was attached to every fibre of my being. The territories between love and sex, which were once so perfectly defined, had begun to collapse. I found myself repelled by every touch that wasn't J's, and I felt nothing when G fucked me. In fact, his caresses would leave me numb and dry—no man has ever left me that dry. I realized only later that what I had begun to feel for him was the opposite of love: contempt. It was sparked off by a chain of events that followed once he discovered I had slept with J, and was besotted by him, and then understood that there had been other men too, and that I had taken his advice about my body being my own to heart.

Over the next two months we began a series of negotiations. He would 'forgive' me my 'sins', as he called them, if only I shared with him each glorious detail. When I refused, on ethical grounds, we proceeded into war. I was cornered into playing defence and I eventually crumbled into a paralytic silence. And all the while, all through this mindless torture, through our alternating peace pacts and blitzkriegs, we continued to end each correspondence with the love cry. The words 'I love you' had become a habit, an involuntary tick. Over the six years we had spent together, we had said it so often that by now it had lost all significance. It had become hollow. It was neither an avowal nor a symptom of some kind of pathological condition of being in love, it was merely a learned habit, like covering your mouth when you cough or saying, 'Excuse Me' when you sneeze; a polite, hygienic, neutral habit, neither good nor bad. We had arrived at a stalemate, but we were both too polite to call it quits, too scared to admit that our love was, in the end, contrary to what we would have liked to believe, neither unconditional nor eternal.

Everything unravelled much like it does in Botton's *Essays in Love* when Chloe finally admits to the narrator that she's been seeing his friend Will. Even before her confession, he had sensed the rupture within their relationship when all the little things she used to find adorable about him suddenly became irritants, and he found himself indulging in acts of romantic terrorism, much like G had begun to do. Botton's narrator, foreseeing the end of his relationship with Chloe, has a disturbing insight about how the thought of the end hangs over every love story, even when it is at its climax. The only difference between the end of love and the end of life, he says, is that at least in the latter, we are granted the comforting thought that we will not feel anything after death. *No such comfort for the lover, who knows that the end of the relationship will not necessarily be the end of love, and almost certainly not the end of life.*

G, in a final fit of rage, emailed me a set of curses:

This is over! There is nothing more to be spoken about this. There is only a past and there is no future. You are a selfish and abhorrent person and I wish no one has to go through the distinct dishonour of having to love you or be loved by you. May you die a thousand deaths at the hands of your shrivelling conscience. I would wish hell on your afterlife, but then that would be too light a punishment for what you are becoming.

I hope you fry in your own juices every day, I hope that your heart turns to stone and that you can't feel a thing. May the numbness spread to your brain and may you never write another word that satisfies you. Every time you have sex or look lustfully at a man or a woman, may your cunt freeze and turn dry. You should live in the daily hell, knowing that you drove the man who made the mistake of loving you to hatred and rage.

By the end of July, I was empathizing with Miller's condition. Down and out in Paris, struggling to survive, he thinks back to the impasse he and his wife Mona (June) had found themselves in. *We came together in a dance of death and so quickly was I sucked down into the vortex that when I came to the surface again I could not recognize the world. When I found myself loose the music had ceased; the carnival was over and I had been picked clean,* he writes in his epic *Tropic of Cancer.*

I was still dying when I met you. I was in a state of trauma. I was struggling with language. The juice that had once flowed so swiftly through my body had indeed been sapped dry. I was empty. But when I met you, in the middle of the monsoon, on that fated day, the second of August, the roots of my being that I was sure had long since withered were suddenly replenished. Some small sliver of life was resurrected. It would take time for me to heal but I found, suddenly, the will to rise from my ashes and renew myself.

({})

In the beginning there was uncertainty. After the first seduction, after the first orgasm, when there was, in my mind, no thought of any continuance, you took it upon yourself to pursue me.

You were supposed to be a one-night stand. A quick fix. A conquest. A ten-line poem in my grand anthology of lovers.

But you had other designs. You seduced me. First with your persistence and later, after I'd relented, with your measured indifference.

In the beginning there was resistance, there were thoughts of escape, as if I had already some inclination of the monumental possibilities of our passion and, threatened by the thought of having to surrender to spiritual bondage, thought it best to flee. But you had already seeped into my system, you had already planted fresh roots, and I found myself incapable of letting you go. You mystified me. Your gait, your charm, your contented solitude, the aura you radiated of being so blissfully unattached to anyone and yet desirous of a dialogue with me. I was convinced your heart was bubble-wrapped and bulletproof, too cautious to yield to the dictates of another and yet, when I confessed to you how deeply you had entrenched yourself under my skin, how you had begun to invade the landscape of my dreams, you made me seem like a coward who was too afraid to let go.

I told you once, over the phone, that I found myself hung up on you. 'It's horrible,' I said. 'I don't want to be hung up.'

'Why is it such a horrible thing?' you said, and for a few moments I was speechless.

'I don't know,' I finally admitted. 'It's you. Your heart is made of lead[4], or some really strong metal. It's bulletproof. You are impossible to penetrate.'

'That's not true. What makes you think that? Give it some time,' you said.

I was in love with you long before I knew it. And when I did, I wasn't sure what to do with the revelation. Neither did you. Often,

[4] When I read this out to you, you corrected me, 'Lead can't be bulletproof. It's a very soft metal; in fact, bullets were made out of lead. The ones that are now banned were called dumdum bullets. You should look it up.' I did. They were called expanding bullets. This is what Wikipedia had to say: 'An expanding bullet is a bullet designed to expand on impact, increasing in diameter to limit penetration and/or produce a larger diameter wound. It is informally known as Dum-dum or a dumdum bullet. The two typical designs are the hollow-point bullet and the soft-point bullet,' all of which made me wonder if you were always made of flesh and if cupid's arrow had lead at its precipice.

it seemed unnecessary to have to articulate it, almost extraneous, so we left it as something unsaid, unspoken, an implicit fact, a given, and we chose not to confront each other with the obvious. We relegated it, instead, to the region of nuance. Occasionally, over an e-conversation, fragments of this 'love cry' would slip. 'Love you', or 'Love' or extensions, like 'Kisses', 'Hugs', but never the whole phrase, always parts, and always on paper or through virtual prisms, never face to face.

Sometimes, when your rhythmic snores signify your fall into sleep, I, still awake, still haunted by the throes of consciousness, gaze at your moonlit face, and I utter the words, but with such practiced softness that no sound ever escapes my lips. I mouth the words and imagine their resonance, but I never allow them to slip past, I do not breathe them into life, and thus, never give you reason to hear my incantation. And yet you often do. And when you do, you do not reply, you do not say a word, you simply reach out for my hand and in the middle of your sleep, kiss the back of my palm, reasserting, through the medium of touch, this skin-communicated thing that exists between us.

({})

The morning after your babbling, I woke up before you, a rare feat considering I get my best sleep after dawn, and I went into the living room to find my moleskine. I set it on the table and dug through my purse for the perfect pen, the one with the thin nib that is just the perfect weight, neither too heavy nor too light, to facilitate a quick long-hand session. I made myself a cup of tea, sat down before the marble-top table, and immersed myself in recounting on paper last night's wine-infused exchange. I was ecstatic. I had spent so much time agonizing about this chapter on love, I was getting nowhere, the subject seemed as elusive as ever, and no amount of reading, no amount of theory could illuminate for me its vagaries. And then we stumbled into conversation last night and everything suddenly seemed to come together, language didn't seem as mucky, and though I knew there was no hope for ordered thought, because the very nature of love resists structural makeovers, I finally had something I could work with.

You emerged from the bedroom about an hour later. It was now around 8 a.m., and you found me busy transcribing.

'Good morning,' you said.

I tugged at your hand, drew you towards me and kissed you.

'What are you up to?'

'Remember that chapter I told you I'd been struggling with? The one on love? Well, last night came as a revelation, and now I have to document it before it gets eclipsed.'

'So you mean I had to perform?' you said.

'I suppose,' I said, and returned your impish grin.

'I'm your guinea pig, am I not?'

'Those are your words, not mine,' I said, citing the same phrase you are known to use when, in jest, I accuse you of crimes like not missing me enough when you're away, or not caring enough about me.

Your glance fell on my cup of tea.

'You made yourself tea but didn't make any for me?'

'I've noticed that whenever you wake up before me, you make yourself tea but don't make any for me, so today I didn't make any for you,' I lied. There was a full cup waiting for you in the kettle on the kitchen counter.

'But that's because you only get up after eight.'

'That doesn't mean I don't want tea,' I teased.

'So if I were to bring you tea, you'd get up?'

'You'll have to find out. Now give me two minutes, I'll get you a cup.'

The next morning I woke up to find your side of the bed vacant. I reached for my phone and checked the time; still 7 a.m. I moved myself to the centre of the bed, so I was in between your side and mine, and fell into a trance-like state of sleep. I woke up to the sound of movement. I could feel your presence hovering over me. I opened my eyes to find you leaning over me, mug in hand. You lowered it towards me, but only so much so that I had to sit up to meet you halfway. You propped a pillow against my back so I could lean against the wall, and then rested the mug within my palms. I said nothing, neither did you. We simply exchanged consensual smiles.

I knew this was a one-time gesture. You were making a point. I savoured the tea, nonetheless. You'd mixed the roasted leaves with a spoonful of Marguerite Hope, a combination I'm not crazy about, but you'd excitedly ordered two tins of each, and we were stuck with them and they needed to be finished.

However, within the next two weeks, you served me 'bed tea' at least six times. Each time felt like a fresh surprise. You also began to pay attention to detail: you'd use the right mug, the one with my name on it, unlike in the beginning, when you'd give me your mug instead. You managed to perfect the brew so it was neither too bitter nor too weak. It is now consistently crisp and smoky.

Each time, you prop the pillow behind my back and leave the mug in my hands, and I look up at you and smile and recite a sheepish 'Thank You'. What I want to tell you, in fact, is that this new little gesture that you've begun makes me fucking joyous. Not because I enjoy being served, in fact, I usually display much resistance towards being pampered in any way but, in part, because this simple gesture always manages to transport me to my childhood when, on mornings when I was either sick or would wake up with a coughing fit, my mother would come to my bed with either a hot cup of tea or eggnog, place it in my hand, and then leave me to finish it. I would sit up and sip the soothing warm liquid and feel it glide down my throat and into my belly, my mind still caught up in sleep, so that the physical act of sipping and swallowing mingled with the psychological act of dreaming and I would find myself lulled by the liquid heat. I'd then place the glass on the floor and fall back into sleep as if I were under a spell.

What I thought was a one-time performance has now become a ritual. And perhaps I am still in that stage of instrumental conditioning when I haven't made the link between your exiting the bed before me and the subsequent offering of morning tea. I still find myself utterly surprised. Part of my astonishment stems from recognizing how this sort of gesture isn't coded into your being. You are not a natural caretaker. In fact, within the dynamics of our relationship, I am the nurturer and you are the one that enjoys being pampered. I am the one giving you hour-long massages and administering to your aches. And I never expected it to be any other way, because I have, since I met you, never wanted to change a thing about you, because for you to change on my account would be for you to no longer be the person I fell in love with, because the who is so indelibly connected with the what, and the what with the who. They are not the distinct categories that Derrida would have us believe them to be. And'absolute singularity', too, is a myth.

It makes me wonder if being in love with someone and being loved by that someone is in fact a process of constant revelations; if one's 'being' is not, in fact, a fixed phenomenological category because at any given time, we are always a subset of multiple selves, never a single, unchanging one. If we are not indeed in a constant state of flux, permanently altering what we believe to be our true selves in relation to the also persistently transforming loved one, we are shedding old habits to acquire new ones, adopting new sensibilities because the previous ones don't harmonize well enough with the loved one's eccentricities.

Our six years together have involved a series of exposures where everyday we come closer to knowing the other's true core. As we continue our individual transformations, spurred by our relentless contact with each other, we mould ourselves to fit against the other, we conceive of new tricks, fresh devices with which to manipulate the other, we navigate the compulsions of our innate proclivities in order to be better versions of ourselves for the sake of the other, we seek out shreds of wisdom from our slew of previous encounters, so that love becomes an ongoing quest towards perfection.

({})

Ours is no mediocre love. There is a tragic monumentality to its passion and dimensions. It exists despite reason or logic or convenience, and it continues to consume us, hold us captive to its whims. It is a love that aspires to reach out to the eternal but the realm of its existence is stubbornly yet exquisitely entrenched in the dictates of the everyday. There is no future in sight; there is only the pronounced absence of any. Ours is a present-tense love. And that is reason enough for its sublimity.

If We Were to Part

I write this from the seat of a rocking chair in your friend K's loft, perched at an elevation of approximately 2,146 metres, in the town of Mashobra. The mountains stretch forth, invading the horizon. Below, at their pit, is a valley where I can see little houses propped against the backdrop of grand pine forests. It is seventeen degrees Celsius, so my weather forecast app informs, in addition to the icon it displays of a dark grey cloud milking raindrops. For the moment, the sky isn't exactly clear, a sheet of clouds looms over, but there are moments when the sun permeates through their fluffiness and shines buoyantly over the mountain peaks. Having spent three days here, I know enough to predict that the skies are temperamental. Yesterday, for instance, when I woke up, the sun dominated the landscape, its rays streaking powerfully through the clouds, drenching the scenery with a precious luminosity. And yet, a few minutes later, I saw the mist parade swiftly through the valley below. Within seconds, it had drawn a veil across earth and sky, and behind this densely white curtain, the clouds had begun to quarrel, while the wind seemed to blow with such force, it felt as though the celestial scaffolding that holds us all in place was about to collapse.

You are, at this moment, in Kanchaburi, at a lower altitude, where the weather also changes quickly. I asked you if it was dramatic, you said it wasn't like in Mashobra. 'You have the mist and the darkening of the light and trees around ... I am on a flattish golf course with mountains at the far end.' You sent me pictures yesterday, and pointed out the rain clouds hovering over the hills of Burma, the land of your ancestors. You are somewhere near the River Kwai, with your recently discovered cousin, and you are looking to cross over into Burma.

For a change, I left two days before you. Which meant you had to administer to your house, ensure things were in place, and I'm quite certain I'll have to deal with most of it upon my return to Delhi. It pained me to not be there for the opening of your show, but I had to do this, I had to escape, I had to finish this handbook. And you supported my decision. You understood, which meant I didn't need to offer you any explanations. I did nonetheless, under pressure from mutual friends who were aghast that I should not be there, and because I was so tempted to stay. It was the same show you were mounting that had first made me fall in love with you, back then, when I had no clue who you were. I saw the show at the National Museum and I fell in love. I had no idea what you looked like in person, whether you were single or attached, or whether I would ever even make your acquaintance. There was something compelling about your way of looking at the world; the domesticity of the everyday and its potential for glory, and at people, lovers, and their private grief. I had this feeling then that these photographs could not have been independent of you, they were so specific to your life, and your personality. And being at the opening would have been like coming full circle, from not knowing you to knowing you better than most anyone else. I would have been a part of that series that dates to the seventies and the eighties, before I was even born. But then, the other morning, a few days before I was to leave, you came into the bedroom and found me splayed upon your bed. The night had been humid, and I'd taken off my shirt, hoping it would be cooler. You had this way of looking at me, and as you exited the room, you made this gesture, as if you were photographing me, you mimed the act of looking into your camera, composing a frame, and immortalizing this moment of nakedness. And that's when I realized that I am already a part of your world and your work.

Over the last few days we spent together, I caught you looking at me constantly, as if you were making mental notes about my body and its movements, archiving them for future indulgence. It reminded me of the second time I had come to Delhi to visit you. The morning I was to leave, you made me eat a bowl of cornflakes and have a cup of tea so I wouldn't starve. You had been sitting across the table from me, and at one point you got up to go to your study. I continued chomping away at the cornflakes, pensive about leaving, but so filled with your scent and your touch, I couldn't but be content. It was a while before I noticed you standing on the sidelines photographing me.

I've come to understand that you are the kind of person that touches the world through your sight. You gaze at things that you covet. I'd often wondered how you could possibly resist touching my dark, naked body lying beside you all sun-kissed and yearning, until one morning I opened my eyes to find you poised towards me, staring at my breasts, and when you noticed I was awake, you ran your fingers playfully over them, as if they were trekking towards a summit.

It is through your eyes that you reveal your lust. When you travel, when you're away for two weeks to a month, what I miss most is the sumptuous feeling of being desired by you, of being the object of your gaze.

({})

The wind has begun to roar. I can hear the cantankerous drops of rain announce themselves on the tin of the roof above me. I have been cocooned inside this loft for more than seventy-two hours, on a bonafide writer's retreat. I spoke to Partho, my unofficial archivist, last evening over Google chat, and I told him how being here in the midst of my solitude compels me to meditate, and I find myself reflecting on the person I've allowed myself to become over these last six years that I have known you. 'You're meeting yourself in the mirror,' he said.

I discovered, among many other things, that you and I are now in possession of a history. Habits have long since leaked between us. We have our own private rituals that individuate our love. Which is perhaps why the fear of what will transpire if we were to part is more pronounced than it ever has been. Our lives have become so intertwined that to extract one from the other seems nigh unthinkable. Like Changez, the Pakistani protagonist in Mohsin Hamid's *The Reluctant Fundamentalist,* notes about his affair with Erica, a fragile woman who is still haunted by the premature death of her first love and finds herself unable to 'be' with him: *It is not always possible to restore one's boundaries after they have been blurred and made permeable by a relationship. Try as we might, we cannot reconstitute ourselves as the autonomous beings we previously imagined ourselves to be. Something of us is now outside, and something of the outside is now within us.*

Two weeks ago we came dangerously close to experiencing the pain of detachment. You'd called me around 6 p.m., asking me to bring you an envelope. There was no trace of urgency in your voice, and so I took my time. When I finally arrived at your house, you were livid.

'Where the fuck have you been?'

'At home, working ...'

'Did you bring the envelope?'

'I did,' and I fished it out from my bag. It was the wrong kind. You wanted the cardboard one.

'I have to send out this package in the next half an hour! Some help you are!'

I rushed over to my place and brought the cardboard one. When I returned I explained to you that you hadn't at all indicated that this was an emergency. I knew not to take offence at your accusation of my being unhelpful. I had spent at least ten hours over the last three days helping you with your funding proposal and, if needed, could compose an entire litany of the many favours I'd done for you over just the last few weeks.

'I tried to call you, why can't you pick up your phone?'

'I was probably in the shower.'

'Just get out. Just go. Leave me alone.'

Ordinarily I would have stayed and calmed you down. But at that moment what was important was for you to have that package dispatched. So I gathered my things and left.

I didn't hear from you at all that night. You ignored my calls and my inquisitive messages went unanswered. I restrained myself from breaking down into grief, all the time believing that what you needed was simply a little space.

I refrained from calling you the next day too, distracting myself with household chores. Occasionally I wept. Steadily, I began to alternate between grief and despair. I decided I would walk by your house that evening and see if you were there so I could explain myself.

Around 8 p.m., I headed out from the back lane that is the shortcut to your house. I cut through the kids' park that serves as a midpoint between your house and mine. I entered your lane and found your car was missing, which meant you were away. Despite having in my possession the keys to your flat, I decided against letting myself in.

Now on the verge of heartbreak, I traced my steps back to the park and instead of exiting and heading back to my place, I found myself walking towards the swings that were, at this late hour, entirely vacant. The park, usually filled with housewives trying in vain to shed years of accumulated cellulite, and the incessant murmur of kids all haloed with the aura of childhood innocence, was desolate.

I rested my sling bag against one of the four poles that bore the weight of the swing, and perched myself on the wooden seat. I raised both my legs so they lay mid-air, parallel to the ground, and placed my palms against the iron loops. Then I pushed myself backwards to initiate movement and as I swung forward, moved my legs downwards to create leverage. After several repetitions of this action, I was oscillating to and fro, and as I moved I began to dwell on the polarities of these two entities. To and fro began to resemble distinct territories and the few stretches of invisible land in between felt like a threshold, a gateway. I wasn't entirely sure what these two spatial masses represented; sometimes they seemed to symbolize my own indecision, my constant back and forth between surrendering to you or abstaining from you because of the inherent dead-end our relationship embodied; sometimes this in-between zone felt like the safety of a terminal where I could momentarily reflect and indulge in the act of waiting for you to decide for me, or to influence my decision; sometimes it felt tainted by the exhausting pathos of displacement that the toing and froing from my house to yours and yours to mine was imbued with, a tiring restlessness because it meant I had to deny myself the privilege of attachment to either residences, leaving me with no claim to sanctuary, and so this mid-point between to and fro revealed itself as a refuge for my exiled state of being.

When I returned to my house, the withdrawal symptoms spurred by the absence of communication with you had begun to set in. I found myself devoid of appetite. I was enraged by your audacity and yet, the threat that always loomed, that one day, you and I, for whatever reason, might cease to be an entity, suddenly became alarmingly real.

I discovered that I had enough strength in me to survive this impending heartbreak. Having been through past loves that had betrayed their inclination towards immortality, I knew I was resilient enough to get over you, to possibly love again, and to even find contentment.

But what frightened me was the breadth of our sensual attachments, and reading the first chapter of the first volume of

Proust's *In Search of Lost Time* or *The Remembrance of Things Past*, seemed to intensify my fear that despite every effort I might eventually make to place you in past tense, the persistence of memory would ensure that you'd keep returning to me like a ghost, because, as science itself has demonstrated, 'the olfactory cortex is embedded within the brain's limbic system and amygdala, where emotions are born, and emotional memories stored, that's why smells, feelings, and memories become so easily and intimately entangled'.

When Proust narrates what has now become an immortal literary experience, his act of eating Petite Madelines with tea, he steers his brilliant first chapter towards a haunting finish with this ominous paragraph:

... But when from a long-distant past nothing subsists, after the people are dead, after the things are broken and scattered, still alone, more fragile, but with more vitality, more unsubstantial, more persistent, more faithful, the smell and taste of things remain poised a long time, like souls, ready to remind us, waiting and hoping for their moment, amid the ruins of all the rest; and bear unfaltering, in their tiny and almost impalpable drop of their essence, the vast structure of recollection.

One of the earliest smells I associate with you is from our first morning together. You had heated water, then poured it into the kettle to make what would be my first Castleton brew. You'd fried eggs, sunny-side up, and placed them on two plates. Then you took a tomato, sliced it into two, did the same with a ripe green capsicum, and placed them both upon the now scalding surface of the same frying pan, in the other corner of which you added four long bits of Pigpo's special pork sausage. You let them sizzle in their collective juices and sprinkled coarse specks of ground pepper. The mad, ravenous scent of pork fat melting against the heat and mingling with the plump tomato juice, the capsicum grazing against the sides of the pan, being scorched by the livid sizzle, causing it to surrender to its outer body all the goodness it had stored within; all of this collided with the humid August air and when I finally tasted the meal you had prepared and partaken of the smoky Darjeeling, I found I had stumbled into a different state of consciousness. I had the distinct feeling of something momentous having occurred inside my body, a contradictory sensation where the act of sating my hunger was awakening in me fresh hunger ... I was beyond satisfied and yet I wanted more, I yearned to sample all the other scents I was certain you had stored within the repository of your kitchen, I longed to add scents from my own repertoire so that we could collaborate to co-create a veritable encyclopedia of the most exquisite tastes and smells.

There were things I had never allowed myself to taste until you coaxed me into it by lecturing me about their innate goodness, their nutritional qualities. Like sprouts. I spent most of my life resisting the raw, crispy, sap-like taste they unleashed upon my palette. But after your having prepared them for me, freshly sprouting them in your kitchen, I find that I can devour a plateful at any hour of the day, and most of all because the taste they bear is so attached to the two-months when I lived with you, during the last quarter of our first year together. Or bitter gourd. You would slice it into rings and fry each piece in oil, keep them aside as you then proceeded to caramelize onion rings. You'd then mix the two humble ingredients together and they would, in a single morsel, become so much more than the sum of their parts; the crispy bitterness of the karela would mingle with the dank brown sugariness of caramelized onion, and for someone whose palette is already predisposed towards the unity of savoury and sweet, the combination proved irresistible. Or the simplicity of bread and butter, the very thought of which makes me salivate. We enjoy breaking bread together, and I remember how once you actually brought back a slice from a larger loaf of sour dough bread all the way from London just because you so wished that I should participate in the experience of having tasted it and of having known the pleasures of sourness and the magic of yeast. And lest we forget the peatiness of single malt that I am indebted to you for introducing me to. I was never one for whisky. The first time I stepped past the threshold of your house, you kept my bags in the bedroom while I surveyed the insanity of your interiors that displayed every symptom of the pathological condition of hoarding, you led me into the living room that shares its space with the kitchen, sat me down on the divan, and asked me if I'd like a drink. I was, like I told you, still a victim of the ex-lover's acts of romantic terrorism, and I had never felt so much relief at leaving Bombay and being in Delhi. You poured me a glass of Laphroaig, and when I took the first sip, was overcome by the liquid smokiness, the golden scent that bore evidence to its maturity, its having lived for at least twelve years in a state of situ so that one day its patience might be savoured by the tongue of an elegant alcoholic. Every sip of single malt I have ever had since then has always born a singular memory: of having finally arrived home.

The monstrous thing about memory is that it is involuntary, that try as we may, we cannot extinguish its potent ability to invade our present without any prior notice, it lurks within our subconscious like a beast that can strike at any given moment without our having to incite it, rendering us powerless against its assault. Even the loss of memory or the inability to remember incidents at will, except for mere disconnected fragments, is nothing short of tragic. Memories that were born of beauty can turn sour if the circumstances devolve, and the memory of a memory creates a fresh memory so that what we have is a multiplication of memories.

That night, empty and forlorn, with yet no word from you, I found myself in mourning. Not because I had lost you, I knew you would eventually come around, and as long as I had your key, I had access to your life. But I grieved at the thought of all that would forever be lost to me if you and I were to end whatever there is between us. Red wine, Bourbon, Darjeeling tea, Goan sausages, Monaco jeera biscuits, cheeses of every kind, even blue cheese—which you hate, because I will always remember that you never had the taste for it—Kakaji potato chips, peanuts, cold cucumber soup, buttermilk, lime juice, Old Monk, pesto, pasta, raspberries, muskmelon, mango milkshakes, mutton xacuti, tandoori chicken, Khow Suey, stir-fried strips of yellow and red bell peppers, French beans pan-fried with garlic and pepper, prawn balachao, bacon, porridge, kebabs, croissants, butter ... *You have imbued yourself in everything! No taste or smell is devoid of you, not even the ones that have yet to be sampled.*

Above all else, you nourish the insides of my being with pleasure. And that is what all the sights and smells and tastes represent. You have made yourself the frequent cause of and witness to the intense gratification of my senses. You bring meaning to all that I experience, because in the retrospective act of sharing it with you or recounting it to you, it becomes something more, it is ameliorated, enhanced and archived. It is through you that I convert my most moving experiences into memories.

And though I mourned, prematurely, the impending loss of my sensual connection to all that is delicious and good because their raison d'etre is you, I will not regret, should we come to pass, the immensity of these memories we will have created. I will not wish they could somehow be erased. I will not, like Eloisa in Alexander Pope's poem 'Eloisa to Abelard', crave the 'eternal sunshine of the spotless mind'. I will simply learn to live in exile as love's refugee.

The next morning, after yet another unsuccessful attempt to reach you, I sent you a slew of messages informing you that through your silence, you were mocking me, inflicting my routine with undertones of misery, that your sarcastic statement about me not helping you enough was far from the truth. To put things in perspective, I reminded you that I'd spent the last two weeks helping you in innumerable ways and yet, there were just three things I had asked of you in return: to bring over the extra swivel chair lying in your office that you had promised me months ago, to take a mug shot of me that I could use when I contributed to magazines, and to spare half an hour for me so I could speak to you about this handbook. You had done none of these.

Then I slipped back into silence, making it clear that the next move had to be yours.

That evening, as I was making myself a cup of tea-bag tea (the way you usually make it when you have no time to bother with the ceremony of brewing, with two tea bags for that extra kick), I heard the door bell ring. Not expecting anyone at the time, I first peered through the peephole. I noticed a figure and was surprised to find it was you. I opened the door and found you out of breath, a swivel chair in tow.

It was only later that I realized you had replied to my earlier message saying you were aware of all that I was telling you, and you knew I was right, but you just needed time to cool off, and that you would start making amends by bringing over the chair.

I let you in and offered you the cup of tea I'd made for myself. Cigarettes were our peace pipe and when you left, I asked if I'd see you again for dinner.

'Let's see, I'll call you.'

Around 8 p.m., with no word from you yet, I decided it was time I made my own peace offering. I took a shower, called a cab, and headed to Defence Colony. I stepped out of the cab and headed straight to Amici and ordered two of their best wood-oven-fired pizzas, and then stopped at the liquor store and bought a Chilean red (I remembered what you once said, 'You can rarely go wrong with a Chilean red').

I had a plan. I would stop by your place and if you weren't in the mood for company, would simply drop off my offering. If you weren't home, I would leave it at your table with a note, and should you want to have dinner with me, we'd find ourselves in an opportune moment. As I was about to get back into the cab, I got a message from you. 'Whiskey and pasta?' I replied, 'Can we do red wine and pizza instead? Coming over.'

You were elated at the sight of the Chilean. You uncorked it enthusiastically and poured the dark red liquid into two of the cutting chai glasses I'd recently gifted you. We sat across the table from each other and gorged on the first pizza, a lovely thin crust with prosciutto and eventually, the second one which had, as toppings, chorizo, rocket leaves and parmesan.

'I realized that this August will mark six years since we've been together.' I said.

'Oh really?' You sounded genuinely astonished. 'Gosh, that's scary!'

'I know! I've never been with someone so intensely for so long.'

'Well, no one is forcing you to stay,' you said, feigning offence.

That night we added new flavours to our growing archive, the holy taste of rocket, the salty-spicy fleshiness of chorizo, and the intense, full-bodied texture of the Chilean red.

Feast

For you the choicest meat: drumsticks, plump ones, from Republic of Chicken. I washed them, made incisions at the intersections between flesh and flesh, and with my bare fingers, I rubbed the marinade so it would seep into the bones. It's an old Goan recipe, African in origin. We call it Cafreal.

I massaged the legs with the marinade and had a sip of red wine. An inconsequential detail, I understand, but red wine does things to me, mixes with my blood, flows through secret pathways in my brain until I finally relent.

For you, no skimping on ingredients, no scrimping with cheese. Crumbled bits of feta sit alone in a bowl. I split a couple of cherry tomatoes into two. They contrast starkly with the crisp white of the goat cheese. I tear some iceberg lettuce, like a writer destroying his masterpiece—calculatingly, so it can be reconstructed in the event of regret. Long slivers of sun-dried tomato. The feta is no longer alone. A drizzle of olive oil, a sprinkling of fresh basil, a few drops of balsamic vinegar. I toss all the ingredients. They jostle for space, they nudge and tug, shuffle and hug, and sigh.

I transport the half-cooked meal from my kitchen to yours, a transfusion of sorts. I stop on the way to buy a bunch of potatoes, just in case, and a quarter-kilo of mostly-sweet black cherries, and one perfectly round musk melon that I could tell was ripe to the core from the effusive, wild scent that hung over the fruit cart, and tampered with the scents of other fruits.

Your kitchen is dysfunctional. The stove is moody, the microwave sings, the toaster regularly goes on strike, and the sink is so low I have to bend to wash the rice which I then soak. Your water heater is the only reliable appliance. I heat two parts of water for the pulao. I use a standard 1:2 ratio. I dice an onion, a large majestic one. It yields to my touch and for the first time in months, my eyes aren't overwhelmed by its pungent perfume. I grate a tomato so that the fattish red fruit is reduced to a wet, thin pulp.

For you, only excess.

Because when you bite into food that is good, your body crumbles. And with every morsel, I dismantle you until you submit to my sliver-of-a-touch.

Because any man who kisses the way you do, with controlled abandon—as if you were transporting a ball of fire from your lips onto mine, as if, with your tongue, you were firmly licking the insides of my soul—is deserving of a feast.

Take my firm black-cherry coloured body. Undress the layers of cloth that surround me like a peel. There are various methods of preparation to choose from. You could have me simmer in the brazen warmth of your touch, or you could use red wine as marinade, to soften me up, leave me intoxicated for hours until I ooze. But tonight, I suggest you eat me raw. Place my unfurled body on an un-made bed, bite into the dark, supple flesh. Start with the nape of my neck until you reach the soft tips of my toes. I strongly recommend you play with your food; let your fingers graze against my nipples, the curve of my belly, the steep incline of my spine. Savour the flavour of my honey-scented skin. Dip into my flesh. Suck on my joints, chew on my bones. Consume me.

For you, a feast.

Artful

I'm still unable to trace exactly when and how this handbook came to be more than a document. I imagine there was a point when some confusion arose. Perhaps I kept referring to it as 'the book' and you assumed it was indeed a book, a work of fiction that I had embarked on. When you started to pester me last year, you asked once again why it was taking so long. I explained that there were many issues I had still to resolve.

'Is it because of me? Am I in the book?'

'You are the book!'

'So what are you so afraid of?'

'Well, you've always been so private about our affair. You've made it clear on many occasions that you'd rather no one knew ... But this book, it's revealing.'

'Women have written about me before, you know.'

'Probably. But this is different.'

'Whatever the reason, I don't understand what's taking so fucking long.'

'Writing is a process.'

'When you started, you said you'd finish it in two months.'

'That was then, when I didn't know better. You can't keep holding that against me. I thought we agreed you wouldn't.'

'I think you're wasting time! I know a lot of writers. When they start on a book, their lives revolve only around the book.'

'We have our methods. Writing doesn't only happen when one is actually writing, it happens all the time. One is constantly making notes, observing things, archiving sensations. In fact, there's no point when a writer is not engaged with the act of writing. It's all consuming.'

'Have you thought about what happens when you finish this?' you asked.

'I'm in touch with this woman, an agent; she represents the India office of this big London agency.'

'What about X? Why don't you get in touch with him?'

'Do you know how many manuscripts he must reject by the hour? There's no way he'd even look at mine.'

'So what? Why should that stop you? What's the point, if you're not going to put yourself out there, test your mettle, see if you stand a chance in the first place?'

I spent the next two days sulking. I don't like feeling pressured into doing things. I prefer taking my time and making decisions intuitively. Besides, I wasn't sure if I was ready to face the repercussions of putting my name to such a book, were it to be published. It was easy for you to harass me about finishing it, given that you hadn't actually read it, save for the harmless, tiny fragments from here and there that I'd read out now and then to amuse you.

The next day, I sat at my desk from morning until late evening and put my chapters into place. Perhaps you were right after all, that I should in fact 'test my mettle', challenge myself, and put this book out there. Now that I had your sanction, I no longer had to fear your reaction. I could spin any opposition from you by reminding you that it was you who had pushed me towards publicity. I wrote to a few publisher friends who read the first three chapters and were intrigued, but not enough to offer me a contract. Their unanimous sentiment was that they'd like to see a finished draft and then come to a decision. Now that I had actually contemplated seeing it published, of immortalizing through printers' ink the complicated snares of our relationship, I needed an external force to have faith in the project. I needed someone to commit to my endeavour. It seemed impossible.

Then one morning, I decided to attempt an email to X. I argued that it wasn't really the risk or gamble I was making it out to be. He would either consent to representing me or would reject the work-in-progress. At the very worst, he wouldn't reply. So I went ahead and composed a little note, enclosing three chapters for him to sample.

He replied within 24 hours and asked if I could tell him more about myself. I can't remember what I said, I have the email somewhere but I'm too embarrassed to reread it. Then he asked if there were more chapters he could see. I sent him a few more, and then, one evening, more than a year ago, when I still lived in Khirki, just as I was about to leave my place to head to you, I found an email from him nestled in my inbox between other, more inconsequential ones. He said he was interested in taking it on.

I was ecstatic.

I rushed over to you and waited until I had you sitting across the marble-top table to break the news. You shared my excitement, but told me to stay calm. We were still in the midst of our conversation when my phone began to ring. It was a UK number, so I decided to pick up.

It was he.

I mumbled as much, that he was actually calling me, but you didn't need for me to tell you, you could fathom from the flushed tone of my voice.

'Relax,' you said. 'Play it cool.'

'Are we on,' he asked.

'Yes,' I said, trying to 'play it cool' but so obviously failing.

'Excellent. So let's drink to it, shall we?'

I was euphoric. You brought out two empty glasses and a bottle of Laphroaig, to ring in the celebrations.

A few weeks later, I emailed you my working manuscript. But of course you didn't bother to read it. What is it with your impatience for the written word? I realized long ago that the only way I can get you to read something is if I read it out to you. I asked you if you'd agree to a listening session. You were all ears. And yet, when I had you across from me, a willing audience, I found I was shy, the contents of the book seemed too intimate for a one-man audience.

'How do you expect this book to be public when you're so shy about even sharing it with me?' you asked.

A few months later I got a call from a musician friend who runs a café in Hauz Khas Village. He asked if I would consider doing a session on the rooftop. I jumped at the idea. Then he asked if there was any way you would agree to showing some of your work there. Strangely, you agreed.

A day before I was to read, you were in a state of panic.

'Listen, what are you going to be reading? How much of me is in there? Am I going to feel uncomfortable? What are the chapters like? How do I come across?' you badgered me.

'I sent you at least ten chapters to read more than six months ago. You should have done your homework!' I said.

'Did you really think I was going to read it?'

'But that was the idea behind the handbook in the first place! You cannot blame me, or worse, censor me at this stage. I'm too far in. If you're going to suddenly start having issues, then I'm fucked, because I won't have a book anymore. And this book needs to be written!'

'Don't worry,' I added, after my rant. 'I won't read anything too incriminating.'

'Thanks!'

The invitation to the reading was rather amusing. On the left-hand corner of the page was a stick figure-like drawing of a girly face, on the opposite end, a gruffy, bearded male counterpart with a camera beside it. The two faces were joined by a wavy cord. I called my friend instantly and asked him to cut the cord in between. It was too obvious and I knew you'd have issues with its representational transparency. He agreed.

That evening I turned up at your house wearing a dress. When we were about to leave, you asked me if I couldn't wear a sari instead.

'You look so elegant in a sari.'

'Why can't you tell me these things beforehand? I don't have a sari with me now.'

'Can't you call one of your flatmates and ask them to get one for you?'

'I can try.'

I did. When we got to Ziro, I found my flatmate, picked up the sari, and went to the loo to change.

You were busy hanging your photographs. I made my way to the rooftop, somewhat nervous and, by now, two beers down.

There must have been about forty people in the audience, mostly friends, my friends. I found my way to the seat that was assigned to me, in a corner of the terrace, diagonal to the crowd. I kept my printouts on the table, and lit myself a cigarette while I waited for everyone to settle down. After a brief introduction, I began my reading. I had chosen to read what I thought were the safest chapters: 'To Strip', 'What I see in You', 'Charter of Demands', and 'Feast'. A friend later remarked they were anything but safe. I noticed you were seated right up front, but the lights were dim, save for the table lamp that I was provided with, and I could barely gauge your reaction. When I was done, I came up to you sheepishly. You were making idle conversation with a curator friend.

'So, are you still talking to me?'

'Of course,' you said. 'Come, have a beer!'

We left soon enough. You had a flight to catch the next morning. All through the ride home, you were unusually quiet. Too embarrassed to make conversation, I kept my thoughts to myself.

We arrived at your place, and I unlocked the door. It was only after we entered that you finally broke the silence.

'I'm hungry. Are you hungry too?'

'I'm not exactly hungry. I had a BLT at Ziro, but I can whip up some pasta if you like.'

'Could you?'

'Of course. Give me twenty minutes.'

'Are you absolutely sure?'

'Yes.'

'You won't later write that I forced you to cook me dinner?'

I was heading to the kitchen when you made this remark. I turned back, startled, and found you grinning ear to ear.

'Very funny!'

I proceeded to prepare the pasta, and when it was ready, decided to wash the dishes so I wouldn't have to do them later. You entered the kitchen just around then and asked if I'd like a drink. I said yes, enthusiastically. You dug through the liquor cabinet and brought out some bourbon and poured us each a glass.

'How's it going with the dishes?'

'What do you mean?'

'I'm just wondering if it will end up in your book.'

You laughed, and I joined in. I was relieved that we were laughing!

Finally, when we sat down to dinner, we spoke about what had just transpired.

'When I came upstairs I felt like everyone was watching me, so I decided to sit right up front. Then, in between, I stuck out my camera and started taking pictures so that I would look busy. It was so bizarre, the whole thing. You were talking about my fridge, my floors, my tap, my plates, my Gypsy. It was all so familiar!'

'And what did you think of it?'

'It's actually quite good. But if there's one critique I have, it's that you could be more critical of me.'

'Oh, I have been! I just didn't read out those parts.'

'So tell me, how does it end? Are they still together, do they break up? What happens?'

'I'm not sure. I think they part ways. There are last words exchanged. She asks him to remember her. It's not a request, it's an invocation, an incantation.'

({})

'The pen and paper are a real impediment if you are seeking relationships that will last,' Kamala Das told her biographer Merrily Weisbord. Kamala should know; she spent most of her life longing to be loved, and embellished each affair with the flourish of her language. Each lover became more than what he were, as if transformed by the fertility of her bounteous imagination. Eventually, Kamala would understand that she had made myths out of men, and the myths were so grand that if they were stripped off, only a skeletal structure would remain. And yet, she couldn't but be seduced by the lure of being desired and desiring, as if this endlessly repeated twin act sustained her writing self like nothing else could. Dr Husain, a Muslim surgeon who awakened her lust in her late sixties, is left speechless when he hears the first piece of text Kamala ever composed about him. 'I am just an ordinary man. Yet, you take this ordinary man and make him great. That is why I love you so much,' he tells her, with Weisbord as his witness.

It's an innocent statement, and yet it alludes to the fact that his love for her rests on her ability to transform his understanding of his own being through her experience of him, imbuing him with qualities he never thought he possessed. By inscribing him in her writing, she elevates him to being not merely the object of her desire but the subject of her art.

Earlier in the book, in Chapter 7, 'I Shall Carry You With

Me', Weisbord, who literally records each word that slips through Kamala's mouth with her handy tape recorder, broaches the subject of the biography. At the time, both writers were supposed to co-create this book that recounts Kamala's life after her controversial *My Story*, particularly the circumstances surrounding her conversion to Islam. Eventually, given her weak constitution and her insane schedules and writing commitments, Weisbord realized it would be a solitary endeavour. In this particular chapter, instead of the usual routine wherein Weisbord travels to Kerala, Kamala makes the journey to Canada as Weisbord's guest. Over tea one morning, Weisbord, slightly perturbed by the situational change, is reassured by an empathetic Kamala that she can indeed ask her anything and she will be militantly honest.

'I came for it, Merrily, I am offering myself,' she says. 'In the time I stay here, you can ask me any question and I will answer. Any awkward question.'

'And we can discuss later if the book is published in Kerala,' Weisbord says.

This question of the future of the book in progress and its context looms over the biography from its conception. Given the conservative backlash that the Nair writer had to face in the aftermath of *My Story*, Weisbord is sceptical about the critical reception of this memoir-of-a-friendship in India.

'It's just that it will make things a bit awkward for me. I also have a family, a sister, brother-in-law, all of them puritanical, not trusting me enough. I keep quiet about my work,' Kamala says.

'I know too well what she means about upsetting family, having censored myself much more than she. I ask if she thinks all memoir writers have the same problem,' Weisbord writes.

'A writer moves away from family, old relationships, very far with the speed of a falling star,' Kamala replies. 'Otherwise, the writer is destroyed, and only the member of the family remains: the mother, sister, daughter, wife. The writer at some point must ask, "Do I want to be a well-loved member of the family? Or do I want to be a good writer?" You can't be both at the same time. These days when you are with the children and are being a very good mother, you cease to be the writer. You feel repelled by the pen and the paper, which are definitely going to come between you and your loved ones.'

Kamala persists with this unorthodox strand of thought: 'The writer might fall in love with someone, she might have a love affair, but if she becomes a total writer within that phase, the relationship will be subtly destroyed.'

'Because the writer can give all of herself only to that task of writing, she will have to write against her loved one, put him under the microscope, dissect him, analyze his thoughts, his words. After a while he is no longer the man you held in your arms at night. You have cut him into little slivers, everything is burst open, he is all seeds and pulp and juice, all spread out in little bits on your writer's table. After that you can't go to his arms the same way.'

'If you are very wise, you try to conceal from the loved one that you know everything about him.'

({})

We work in different mediums, you and I. You see through a glass darkly, while I try to turn flesh into word. What unites us is a shared sensibility towards the process of archiving. You collect fragments of moments that you deem significant enough to be revisited later. As do I. Except you rely on the vicissitudes of light[4] while I depend on the vagaries of my imagination. Though I don't write fiction, try as I may—I find it tiresome to invent characters and plot lines—it is through my imagination that I transform everything I experience into the written word. We are both fighting against the consuming black holes of memory and forgetting; recording, intuitively, all that we know must be memorialized.

In her classic treatise *On Photography*, a book even you have read, Susan Sontag puts it beautifully: *All photographs are mementos. To take a photograph is to participate in another person's (or thing's) mortality, vulnerability, mutability. Precisely by slicing out this moment and freezing it, all photographs testify to time's relentless melt.*

In our attempts to preserve, for imagined eternity, relics of ephemeral moments, we both invade the lives of others. I cut you open on the surface of my writing desk; you pry your way into the private moments of the everyday and steal their souls.

To photograph people is to violate them, by seeing them as they never see themselves, by having knowledge of them that they can never have, it turns people into objects that can be symbolically possessed. Just as a camera is a sublimation of someone, it is a subliminal murder, a soft murder, appropriate to a sad, frightened time.

How do we define the centrality of each other's being when both of us find ourselves solely committed to the supposed purposelessness of art? When experience forms the core of our

[4] I love how you once put it, in the middle of a video interview you were doing with a newfound relative. He, very overtly Christian in his beliefs, asked you if you believed in religion. Nervously, you said, 'I'm a photographer, I work with light, the sun is my God.'

individual practices, when our personalities are so central to how we perceive the world, and possibly each other?

You've often accused me of being two selves—one who is rendered speechless in the throes of a tempestuous conversation, and the other who, after the moment has passed, is able to return to it through the medium of words and frame a frightfully articulate response that betrays any previous exhibition of astonishment.

'Why is it that you are only able to show your strength in your writing? Why can't you be like that when you're speaking to me?' you once asked me.

I found an answer for you in an extract from Volume 1 (1934-35) of Anais Nin's diaries: *The writer is the duelist who never fights at the stated hour, who gathers up an insult, like another curious object, a collector's item, spreads it out on his desk later, and then, engages in a duel with it verbally. Some people call it weakness. I call it postponement. What is weakness in the man becomes a quality in the writer. For he preserves, collects what will explode later in his work. That's why the writer is the loneliest man in the world, because he lives, fights, dies, is reborn always alone, all his roles are played behind a curtain. He is an incongruous figure.*

Despite your complaints about having been reduced to a guinea pig, you have enjoyed this process of being documented; this role reversal where you are the focus of a lens and not the person looking through it. And I admire the grace with which you have surrendered yourself to my gaze; the way you have 'offered' yourself to me as a muse. Within these pages you are the one under observation; you are my subject.

When I brought this to your attention, I asked whether this kind of dynamic had been explored in photography. You placed a book in front of me. *Portrait,* by a Japanese photographer, Seiichi Furuya. On the cover was a haunting frontal black-and-white photograph of a woman who, I would learn when I browsed through the book, was Christine, Furuya's wife and muse. I went through the text, at the end, by Monika Faber.

As Alfred Stieglitz portrayed his life partner, Georgia O'Keeffe, in her endless photographic images, so did Seiichi Furuya with his wife Christine. The only difference lies within the fact that their deep relationship spanned only seven years before her untimely death. In these desperately intimate portraits, the viewer follows Furuya's growing understanding of the many sides of his deceased wife but also opens a window into understanding himself. As stated by the artist, 'As I see her, take photographs of her, look at her in the pictures, I find myself.' An amazing example of the camera's ability to portray the soul of both its subject and the photographer.

I also stumbled upon this revealing line by Stieglitz from a letter he wrote to O'Keeffe in 1918—'All I want is to preserve that wonderful something which so purely exists between us.'

I read Furuya's statement within Faber's text as something of a confession, and I speak of confession in a Catholic sense where contained in the admittance is a trace of guilt, of having committed a sin. Going through Furuya's photographs one cannot but be overwhelmed by the absolute potency of the act of looking, the shameless intensity of photographing his wife in all her naked and clothed glory, of seeking her out in private moments, prying on her, and recording these acts of intimacy. You imagine him so besotted by her that any trace of light falling on her skin is enough to inflame his artistic frenzy. His gaze upon her is redolent of love. You imagine that this is about her, about immortalizing her beauty and her vulnerability, her fragility, her mortality, and then he confesses that as he takes photographs of her, looks at her in the pictures after she is gone, he finds himself!

In another note, in 1979, he reiterates: *If you consider the taking of photographs to be in a sense a matter of fixing time and space, then this work—the documenting of the life of one human being—is exceptionally thrilling ... in facing her, in photographing her, and looking at her in photographs, I also see and discover 'myself'.*

In the case of Stieglitz, it was O'Keeffe who survived him, and it was she who curated for publication the first set of photographs of herself taken by him. 'It was the person looked at, not the person looking at who found her vis-a-vis in years or decades of old pictures,' Faber remarks.

In 1978, O'Keeffe had this to say about the experience of revisiting those portraits. 'When I look over the photographs Stieglitz took of me—some of them more than sixty years ago—I wonder who that person is. It is as if in my life I have lived many lives.'

Faber assesses O'Keefe's statement: *Due to the long time that passed, there is a gap between the experience she's made herself and the outward expression; her idea of her own state of being at a certain moment that is long past, and the evidence provided by the picture do not correspond to each other. The absent creator of the photographs, Alfred Stieglitz, cannot be asked about these pictures as a life partner, he remains first and foremost an artist.*

({})

I must not pretend it is you alone I have been documenting. This handbook is, to remind you of the epigraph at the beginning of this handbook, a Barthesian version of a dedication. *An episode of language which accompanies any amorous gift whether real or projected, and more generally, every gesture, whether actual or interior, by which the subject dedicates something to the loved being.*

Which makes me the subject, and you the recipient of my offering. And yet, this dedication would have been impossible had you not first made an offering of yourself, had you not submitted yourself to my scrutiny, had I not been permitted to archive our exchanges, make relics of our intimacies.

The initial impulse, to chronicle for you a simple history of past lovers and a map of my body with places to visit, has changed. The need for either has been rendered redundant. This handbook has become uncontainable, it has assumed a life of its own, as if, in the act of writing, some force external to me was moving my fingers in directions I didn't originally chart out, navigating me through twists and turns I'd in fact hoped to avoid.

'Is it all true?' X had asked me over the phone after having read the first ten chapters.

'I'm afraid it is,' I said, 'all of it,' not sure whether this was what he wanted to hear.

We have both been implicated; we have both been inscribed.

Somewhere along the way, your status changed from 'inconvenience' to inevitability; from 'a disruption to my state of being', to its elemental constituent.

Embossed within these pages are fragments of our individual truths. Mine were revealed to me in the process of writing. Sift through the margins and you'll find yourself too.

Retreat

During an interview with a religious, newfound Burmese relative, you were asked if you believed in God.

'I'm a photographer. I believe in the sun,' you had said instinctively.'It comes up unfailingly every morning,' you explained, suggesting, almost, that the sun, with the certainty of its presence, was god enough for you. While religious evangelists would argue that the sun exists because 'God' exists, you would probably say that light exists because the sun exists, and that god's existence is irrelevant to that of the sun.

You are not a man of faith.

Faith is unconditional. It is not contingent on certainty. As the resurrected Christ said to his disciple Thomas, who refused to believe he had appeared to the others, not until he could witness first-hand the stigmata left by the nails, put his finger into those dented pockets, and thrust his hand into Christ's side, 'Reach hither thy finger, and behold my hands; and reach hither thy hand, and thrust it into my side: and be not faithless, but believing.' When Thomas finally did believe, Christ said unto him, 'Thomas, because thou has seen Me, thou hast believed:

blessed are they that have not seen, and yet have believed.'[5]

You may believe in the sun when it isn't shining, but your belief comes from knowledge, not faith.

({})

Until very recently, I did not have faith in you.

'How does it end,' you had asked me after my reading at Ziro.

'I'm not sure,' I replied. 'I think they part ways. There are last words exchanged. She asks him to remember her. It's not a request, it's an invocation, an incantation.'

({})

Until the sixteenth Century, when Copernicus first proposed the heliocentric model suggesting that the earth revolved around a statutory sun, mankind believed otherwise. The Ptolemaic system governed philosophy. The Earth was assumed to be the orbital centre for all other celestial bodies. Until Copernicus' model came to be accepted, the phenomena of sunrise and sunset must have been perceived as mythical, just like rainbows were seen as a covenant between God and man. That we continue to speak of the sun as moving across the horizon, as rising in the East and setting in the West, is an indication of how much currency we place on our perception of cosmic phenomena, when in fact our entire experience of solar light is an optical illusion.

The sun doesn't actually rise or set. The illusion is caused by

[5] John 20:27, King James version

our vantage point; by our being situated within a rotating reference frame.

({})

'What are you working on?' you asked me last week.

'I'm trying to understand sunrise and sunset.'

'What's there to understand? It's about the quality of light. It's that time when the sun is parallel to the horizon. There's a lowness in the angle, there's a warmth of colour.'

'I'm trying to fathom its mythic dimensions. The fact that it's an illusion, and yet it really does seem like the sun is either rising or sinking.'

'Well, doesn't it have a fairytale trope to it?' you said.

'What do you mean?'

'That whole idea of walking into the sunset being a metaphor for a happy ending ...'

'I didn't think of that! You're right!' I said.

I looked it up later. According to the Cambridge Dictionary, to 'ride, drive, walk, etc. (off) into the sunset' is 'to begin a new, happy life at the end of a story'.

I even found this quote by George Lucas: 'If the boy and girl walk off into the sunset hand-in-hand in the last scene, it adds ten million to the box office.'

({})

I spent at least five hours this weekend rediscovering the 1995 BBC-produced episodic version of *Pride and Prejudice* starring

Colin Firth and Jennifer Ehle. It remains one of the most faithful adaptations of Jane Austen's epic novel about Mrs Bennet's unenviable predicament of having to find suitable husbands for each of her five daughters in a time when women were considered property and were therefore not allowed to inherit any. Since you were away in China, we resumed our WhatsApp thread. 'My head is so filled with thoughts of Mr Darcy,' I said over a text. 'Mr Rocheshter, Mr Knightly, and Mr Darcy... my idea of the perfect man has always been a combination of these three literary personalities,' I explained. 'As for me, I always aspired, however unsuccessfully, to be a combination of Rosalind from Shakespeare's *As You Like It*, and Elizabeth Bennet.' When we spoke over Skype the next day, you asked in an grouchy, over-possessive tone: 'Who is this Mr Darcy? Is he a real person or a character from a book?' I was both amused and amazed. 'He's a fictional character,' I said. 'You come closest to being him ... Have you never heard of him?'

'I don't read, so I don't know,' you explained, sheepishly.

If you were here, across the table from me, I would have told you how I think *Pride and Prejudice* is perhaps one of my favourite fairytales. You would have asked me why I thought it was a fairytale. I would have told you it has all the elements of one: a fairy godmother-like personage (Mrs Gardiner), an evil stepmother prototype (Lady Catherine), along with an evil stepsister-like character (Miss Bingley), with Darcy as Prince Charming. Except Darcy is not conventionally charming in any way, and Elizabeth is too level-headed to believe in happy endings, at least not for herself. She doubts Darcy from the very beginning, even though he is taken in by her almost immediately after they first meet. His fatal flaw is his pride. Hers is her prejudice. It is only when each of the two lovers has learned to swallow these ego-impelled weaknesses that they can be equals.

The line that stayed with me, though, after reviewing the film and re-reading the book was what Elizabeth says to the irate Lady Catherine, Darcy's aunt, who, irked by rumours about Darcy's impending proposal to Lizzie, which would go against his intended destiny—marrying her daughter—rushes to communicate her dissatisfaction about the affair. When Lizzie refuses to promise to reject any proposal Darcy may make, she calls her an 'unfeeling, selfish girl.'

'Do you not consider that a connection with you must disgrace him in the eyes of everybody?' she says.

'Lady Catherine, I have nothing farther to say. You know my sentiments.'

'You are then resolved to have him?'

'I have said no such thing. I am only resolved to act in that manner, which will, in my own opinion, constitute my happiness, without reference to you, or to any person so wholly unconnected with me.'

It is this declaration that makes Elizabeth one of the most powerful literary figures I've encountered. It is her rebellious resolution to act in the interest of her own happiness that sets her apart from her many fictional counterparts. It is from her that I draw the strength to continue to be with you despite rational opposition that insistently reminds me of the difference in our ages that makes you so unsuitable.

One evening, when we were sufficiently intoxicated with fine wine and sumptuous food, I dared to ask you, rhetorically, what you would have done without me. It was a reaction to some incident where I had come to your rescue, to either remind you of something you had forgotten or to retrieve something you had possibly misplaced.

'What would you do without me?'

'I would have continued as before,' you answered. 'I wouldn't have known otherwise.'

Like Darcy, you too cannot 'fix on the hour, or the spot, or the look, or the words, which laid the foundation' of your love for me. 'I was in the middle before I knew that I had begun,' Darcy tells Lizzie when she later, playfully, asks him to recount the chronology of his affection for her.

I doubted you from the beginning. I mistook your regard for me as a passing fancy, as a temporary occurrence that would eventually grow faint. I cannot remember when I surrendered to you. I have acknowledged earlier my resistance to pursuing whatever was evolving between us because I was afraid it would turn out to be one-sided. You wouldn't have it. You challenged me at every turn, you made it seem as if for me to step away would be an act of cowardice.

'Where is this heading?' I asked you once, somewhere around the third or fourth month of our relationship.

'Let's just take it one day at a time and see where it goes?' you said.

And here we are, on the brink of our seventh year together. Here we are, still with no destination in sight.

While our circumstances remain the same, what has changed is the fact of our faith. We no longer doubt how strongly we feel for each other. We do not indulge in daily utterances of the love cry. There is no longer any trace of angst that would otherwise impel us to make such professions. It is not the knowledge of the other's passion that inflects our certainty. It is faith.

({})

And yet, there are moments when I fear that we too shall pass. My age does not permit me to dream of a future with you. I hesitate to. I am told by friends that turning thirty changes you. I am a year and a half away from that milestone; you have two years left before you turn sixty. Our cultural contexts do not allow us to believe in happy endings. I fear that one day in the near future I may either have a sudden epiphany of the futility of our relationship or might meet a more suitable partner, someone from my generation with whom I can envisage a more settled situation, even while I convince myself that I, in my conceited independence, am not interested in conforming to the dictates of marriage.

Perhaps there will come a day when I come before you, not to indulge in your company, but resolved to seek finality.

'Is this how it ends?' you will ask.

I will have no answer. I will shrink into my new relationship with all the enthusiasm I can muster and begin the process of forgetting you, of placing you in past tense, of converting you into an old flame and finally, of instituting you within my expanded encyclopedia of ex-lovers.

Love's fatal flaw is that it comes with no warranty. There is always the threat of expiration. There is always the danger of falling out of it, or no longer seeing in the loved one all the qualities that singled him out in the first place, that made him so alarmingly unique. There is the fear that one day, affection may turn into resentment, love may be replaced by contempt. The only certainty there is in the world as we know it is that the sun will continue to rise and set and rise and set again the next day and the day after until one day, some billion years later, it too will quietly combust and self-destruct, shedding all illusions of permanence.

({})

Should we come to pass, is it possible somehow to ensure resonance? Our love will have had its fair share of witnesses, but what of its testimony? Can it withstand the natural process of erasure that is forgetting? Stephen Dunn in his melancholic poem, 'The Vanishings', prophesies that 'Every other truth in the world, out of respect, / slides over, makes room for its superior.'

One day there'll be almost nothing
Except what you've written down,
then only what you've written down well,
then little of that.

...

It's vanishing as you speak, the soul-grit,
the story-fodder,
everything you retrieve is your past,
everything you let go
goes to memory's out-box, open on all sides,
in cahoots with thin air.

Sometime after 'If We Were to Part', I retreated from this handbook. It was not a conscious decision. It was not an act of surrender. It was inescapable in hindsight, involuntary. I stepped back. I withdrew. I stopped documenting our every conversation. I stopped dissecting you on my writing table. I ceased to fill my moleskine with my momentary insights. For the first time since I had met you and known you, I indulged in the gesture of being. I engaged with the presentness of our time together. Our private moments were no longer fodder for my imagination.

I used to be afraid that you were more muse than lover. I used to fear that my love for you wouldn't outlive your function as a character within these pages. Ever so often I would find myself apprehensive about my motives. Was I with you because I loved you? Or was I with you because you were my subject? Was I in love with you because you were a perfect muse? If so, then would I continue to be in love with you after I had committed you to writing? These were not permanent misgivings but passing afflictions, lapses in passion that I would only articulate to myself in the quiet hours of night when I was home alone or struggling with sleep.

While this handbook became, without our knowing it, a document of our trajectory, one day it may serve as a relic. It has already evolved into an archive of lived moments. When I read you excerpts, I find I am more astonished than you, about all that passed between us, about everything that has already morphed into the past.

During my stay at the retreat I found myself forgetting details. I had become inattentive. I was present, always, but I had managed to quell the voice inside my head that is otherwise constantly translating the moment and inscribing it in words. I had let go. I had learned to resist the urge to document. I now knew how to repress the impulse to archive.

I'm able to trace the beginnings of this new tendency to the time we first achieved equanimity, or homeostasis, to use a medical term. It was during the end of our fifth year together and the start of our sixth. I was to turn twenty-eight. I urged you to spare a week to go away with me to Goa, the land of my origins. I documented nothing of those five glorious days. They were perfect and windswept and redolent of monsoon's wetness and fertility and the scent of your breath hovering over my nakedness and the mind-altering ecstasy of a grand, long-overdue fuck. We let ourselves go. We yielded to each other.

You gifted me three books by Orhan Pamuk and a bottle of Russian Standard. I started on the thickest one immediately. I remember lying on the four-post double bed amidst the trill of pouring rain. You were busy working, and that's why we had chosen to be in Goa, because we had each been there so many times before, there would be no pressure to explore, and so we could simply be, without the urgency of having to discover anything except each other, while continuing to attend to our daily routines. It was on my birthday that I embarked on the 728-page book that would lead to my undoing.

I do not need to recount for you the plot of *The Museum of Innocence*. You passively read the novel with me. It was rather wonderful, the newfound obligation I had been entrusted with, of recapping for you the story as it unfolded. Each time I'd put the book down to take a break or continue with other engagements, you'd ask if anything new had transpired. It isn't the kind of book featuring spine-chilling twists at every alternate chapter. It's a slow-paced novel. Kemal doesn't love Fusun, he fetishizes her, he is fixated, and when he realizes he cannot have her because of his own stupidity, he starts to collect any and every object he can find that has been animated by her touch or that relates to his memories of her. He becomes, over time, the anthropologist of his own experience, and finally, when he outlives her, converts her parents' house where he spent 409 weeks, visiting them for supper 1,593 times, into a museum filled with all the objects he had collected as a consequence of his obsession with her: *I had only to see them once and I could remember the past Fusun and I had shared, the evenings we had spent together at the dinner table. I had associated each and every object with a particular moment, and as the years passed, it seemed as if these remembered moments expanded and merged into perpetuity.*

Pamuk threw me off my game with his meticulous eye for detail. My handbook seemed almost futile in its scope and intention after I was done with his novel. And then, as if to further mock me, Pamuk actually opened a Museum of Innocence, breathing life into his fiction, so that the ticket printed on page 713 of my copy can now actually be used to gain entry.

I paused. The handbook came to a standstill. I felt no great compulsion to record our moments, or your gestures, or things you would say in passing that you'd think nothing of, but which I would have otherwise stopped to collect for future reference. For a while I even questioned if what I felt for you was love or if you were merely a victim of my obsession.

Then one day in September, I found myself rummaging through my bag in search of my moleskine. The impulse had returned.

Just that morning, around 10 a.m., when we were stirring out of our sleep, you turned towards me.

'You were so drunk last night!' you said.

There was no denying it. It was the first time I'd ever thrown up after getting back home.

'I'm really sorry,' I said. 'The thing is, I didn't feel drunk. It's that Afghani food we ate before we drank.'

'It's okay, baby. It's okay to get drunk once in a while.'

'Weirdly enough, I feel so good today! I feel like I've got everything out of my system.'

'Well, we brought back some takeaway last night so you can put it back in your system at lunchtime.'

Laughter.

Pause.

'You were so drunk you were yapping away in the car on our way back!' you said to my mortification.

'More than usual?'

'Yes! Do you not remember any of it?'

'Of course I do!'

I lied. I didn't. I remembered fragments. As we were having breakfast, you decided to quiz me about what I could recall. I knew it was a jibe, you had noticed lately that I was beginning to forget many little things, small tasks and little promises. When I'd confess that it was not always possible to remember everything all the time, you said I was wrong. 'Just don't forget!' you advised, as if it were really that simple.

'So what do you remember?'

'I remember telling you that you ought to gift me a print of one of your photographs. I argued that if you took the bulk of all the many little assignments I've done for you, like writing your proposals, editing your bios, helping you with your catalogues, and if you measured it in terms of billable hours, it would exceed the worth of a single print. In other words, you should gift me a print. You challenged me and told me to make a spreadsheet listing these assignments and then we'd talk.'

'Do you know what else you said?' you intervened. 'You said [mimicking me], "This book will immortalize you!" Do you remember?'

'Of course!' I said, though honestly it was only when you reminded me that I felt the full import of my audacity.

That afternoon the voice inside my head started speaking to me once again. I wrote 'Artful', I added 'Feast', and in a few days, sent the manuscript to X and waited.

I was nervous. I wasn't sure if he would like what I had written. For two days there was silence. On the third day, I had a strange dream. I was lying on a surgical table. Two doctors, one male, the other female, were gazing at my vagina, examining it with their expert eyes. They seemed confused. They called in a third expert, a man who seemed like an unconventional medical professional. He peered at my vagina and was astonished. I had this out-of-body experience where I felt I could, in my technicoloured dream, see the glowing pink flesh that he was looking at. 'It's the most beautiful vagina I've ever seen,' he said.

That evening, X replied. 'Extremely well written, almost French in tone somehow and wholly original. Really, I see it as a love letter to PB.'

'How does it end?' you asked when I shared with you the news of X's reception of the manuscript.

'With a bunch of telegrams, the ones I sent you just before India shut down its telegraph division. I thought it fitting that a book that is written in the epistolary tradition should end with a dated means of long-distance communication. I managed to get the department to transmit such scandalous things. If only they knew.'

({})

'Remember Me.' These two words were my first text to you the night after we first met. It was meant as both an intercession and an inquisition.

'I remember you already,' that was my fourth text to you, after you had returned to Delhi, and it prompted this reply:

'Sweetie, you are my dearest. xxP'

Even now I remain obsessed with memory. It's like some symptom of a pathological fear of forgetting and of being forgotten. As if our relationship will have had no significance if it is somehow not remembered or if it passes callously into oblivion.

'Blessed are the forgetful, for they get the better even of their blunders,' Nietzsche wrote in *Beyond Good and Evil*, a line that found utterance in Michel Gondry's 2004 film, *Eternal Sunshine of the Spotless Mind*. As Joel's subconscious goes into battle mode when it realizes his memories of Clementine are being erased, he lets out this plea: 'Please let me keep this memory, just this one.'

Perhaps my fixation with the subject of memory stems from my fear of your proclivity towards forgetting; a consequence of your having lived thirty years more than I; of having, in the course of these years, experienced more than you are able to consciously process. My pathological fear of your forgetting is what led me to write this handbook. And yet I find that while the act of writing may have resulted in an archive for the reader, for me, it has entailed a process of erasure. So much has transpired between us that when I return to this book and re-read its contents, I find myself amazed by all that these pages have recorded, so much of which I no longer remember as conveniently.

This memoir of our love is being forgotten even as it is being written.

'How does it end?'

'I don't remember.'

({})

All my friends who are members of my generation are suddenly either married or betrothed. It occurs to me that I am alone in my reticence against the social institution. When Partho indulged me over the phone with details of his impending proposal to his longtime girlfriend (he was to pop the question while the two were sailing on a yacht), I saw my future as the sole unmarried one in all my immediate friend circles. It occurred to me in that moment that you and I have been involved with each other much longer than most of these now-married couples. Our relationship predates almost all of theirs. And yet, given our reluctance to conform to any such social pressure, our relationship is beginning to seem illegitimate.

'It's just a matter of form,' Partho said when we were trying to understand the rationale behind the concept of marriage in contemporary times.

While the Supreme Court of India recently expanded its

vocabulary to include live-in relationships within the purview of its legislation, our arrangement doesn't satisfy any of its norms. Though we may be members of the opposite sex and therefore are not victims of its unimaginative and regressive stand on Article 377, we do not cohabit the same space, preferring instead to continue with our separate residences. We also have no joint bank account or proof of shared finances. The law was meant to protect women, and strangely, the summary in one of the newspapers says this: 'Entrusting the responsibility, especially on the woman to run the home, do the household activities like cleaning, cooking, maintaining or upkeeping the house, etc., is an indication of a relationship in the nature of marriage.' Perhaps that's the only logical way we could be construed to be akin to man and wife. I look after your house in your presence and absence.

However, my excuse for taking upon myself the responsibility of your mess, I've come to realize, is utterly selfish. For some absurd reason, it is when I am slaving away with your dishes or your floors that I find myself most attuned to my inner self. Thoughts gleam like sparkling soapsuds. Insights rush through me like wild water gushing through your rusty faucets. With each sweep of the mop, with each erasure of grime off your marble floors, I find myself transported from the monotony of the everyday into a more transcendental space. I feel as if something were communicating through me, like I was the medium and some more divine force was dictating the words, many of which formed the script of this handbook.

It was sometime in October that it dawned on me that part of the reason for my involuntary retreat from writing was the unintended consequence of my having employed a maid. She was wonderful and efficient and had consented not only to administer to my household chores but to also take care of yours. I no longer needed to cook and clean. She handled everything. Over the few months I had the privilege of having her, I lost my touch with food along with the contact I had always enjoyed with my private thoughts; not the stream of consciousness kind that is always going on in one's head, but the more reflective kind that converts experience into language, when light bulbs go off in the brain like a chain reaction. Like Henry Miller once said: *After all, most writing is done away from the typewriter, away from the desk. I'd say it occurs in the quiet, silent moments, while you're walking or shaving or playing a game, or whatever, or even talking to someone you're not vitally interested in.*

My writing is entrenched in the domesticity of our passion. This handbook is inspired by the kind of kitchen-sink realism that is at the crux of our love.

Had you not left me your keys, had I not entrusted you with a spare copy of mine, we would never have survived.

We occupy separate habitats that are located within a convenient three-minute space, affording us the perfect amount of proximity and the right amount of distance. Both are home enough for us.

We have, in the span of seventeen months, established a routine. When we are both in Delhi, we convene every evening over red wine or single malt at your house. I either transfuse your kitchen with dinner I cooked in mine, or I start from scratch, at your house. We revel in each other's company and finally dissolve into sleep, arms and legs entangled like creepers. When we wake up to freshly brewed tea, I preside over the breakfast ritual, we read the news on our tablets, exchange details of our individual schedules for the day I do the dishes, change into whatever I was wearing the previous evening when I'd come over, and take my leave. I come up to you in your office and tell you I'm off. You walk me to the door and kiss me on my mouth. After several warm hugs, we part ways. I return home, make myself a second cup of tea and begin my day, knowing that in a matter of hours, after the sun has set, we will be in each other's presence once again.

Home is a question of form. Our arrangement, though unusual, is not unique. When I visited the Montparnasse cemetery during my stay in Paris, I found it rather endearing that Sartre and Simone perhaps only began living together after they were no longer alive. They occupy the same six feet of earth and their names and timelines have been etched on the same tombstone. During their fifty-year-long relationship, they kept their individual residences. In fact, Sartre lived in a high-rise on Boulevard Raspail that overlooked the very cemetery where he would eventually be buried. Simone lived in the immediate vicinity. There's a clip from a 1967 documentary on Sartre where he stands in the balcony of his apartment and points her to where his friends lived. 'There, in that house, lives my mother. And there lives Castor in the white house.' Castor was Simone's nickname. The voiceover reveals to the audience their routine for the last thirty-six years: 'Every morning they work separately.'

When I left Delhi to meet my family for Christmas, I missed our home more than ever. I felt displaced. I knew I would have to deny you, yet again. I would have to, for the sake of maintaining the Yuletide spirit, repress any mention of you that would either arouse their curiousity or incite them into lecturing me, all the time telling me that their intentions stemmed from their concern about the interests of my happiness. 'Your parents love you so much,' my sister-in-law whispered in my ears when I was leaving to go to Kerala to attend a close friend's wedding. 'Don't break their hearts.' It was a melancholic moment for me, that departure, given that I have finally accepted the fact of my parent's mortality. We had managed to spend yet another Christmas together, the whole family, and somehow, when I was leaving, I felt as though I was breaking free from my family's hold over me; I was stepping away from the power of their influence over my life's decisions. Later, I remembered something my professor at University once said to me, 'If you're going to worry about family and about what they're going to think, you have no business writing.' I was more emotional than I had imagined I'd be. I hugged each one with a sense of finality, as if I would never again return to them. I held my mother and father like a bride would on the eve of her wedding, knowing that she could never again return to the home of her childhood, fully aware that this home would now only exist in her memory, and that she had to conceive a new one; for that is where the notion of home truly exists, not in a physical structure but in the boundless confines of the individual imagination.

When I was about to board my flight to Kerala to attend a friend's wedding, you were still unsure where you would be on New Year's Eve. Not a big fan of this particular festivity, I kept my own plans unfixed. I told myself that what I wanted most at the cusp of the new year was to be home, which would be rendered impossible if you were going to be away. Just minutes before I could be bussed to my flight, you messaged saying it turned out you would be in Delhi after all. The next morning, when I finally arrived at my destination; a guest-house overlooking the Payamballam beach, you called and we discussed return flights. After some research conducted purely from your end, you messaged to tell me you'd booked me a flight and had even confirmed my seat.

On the morning of the 31st, I took the 7 a.m. train from Kannur to Kozhikode. When I arrived, an hour and a half later, I took a cab to the Calicut airport and waited to catch my 1.30 p.m. flight, which was delayed by an hour. You called to ask what time I'd reach Delhi. It turned out the Air India flight would first land in Coimbatore, then Mumbai, finally landing in the Capital at 8.30pm. You apologized. You didn't know I would have to endure such such a long-winded itinerary. I told you I didn't care how long it took, as long as you were on the other side of my journey.

I arrived in Delhi and took a cab to my house. You were still in your office in Noida and couldn't be there in time to welcome me. I switched on the lights (*Home is where you can find the light switch unerringly in the dark,* wrote I. Alan Sealy in *Red*), I tuned in to a Bossa Nova radio station, put on the geyser, strolled in my suitcase, and took a shower. Half an hour later, the doorbell rang. I opened the door to find you and within seconds we were both home.

You fixed us a drink. Laphroaig. We sat in the living room in the midst of the music. I gave you the late birthday gift you wanted, two kilos of Parmesan cheese. We cut off a small chunk from the larger whole and relished the specks of rock salt we encountered with each bite.

'I need to go back to my place, it's a mess,' you said.

'What kind of mess? Does it have to be dealt with today?'

'I had to move things around. I was looking for something.'

'Let's finish our drink and then leave. I'll come with you.'

'Are you sure you don't want to go to your friend's party?'

'I'm too exhausted to make small talk with strangers. Besides, there's no other place I'd rather be tonight.'

We left soon enough. Three minutes later we were in your kitchen discussing our dinner options. We had decided upon pasta as we fixed ourselves another round of Laphroaig.

Within an hour we were sitting across from each other on the marble-top round table with our pasta and our single malt and slivers of Parmesan. In the middle of our meal you got up, enticed me to get up too, and when I was standing, you put your arms around me and held me tight.

'Happy New Year, babes.'

'Happy New Year, love.'

And just like that, we ventured into 2014.

({})

This morning, after a week of hurried Skype calls that were always interrupted because of faulty networks, we managed a full-length conversation over the phone. We were finally in the same time zone. You were back from China, except you were now in Chennai. Yesterday you made the presentation on your photojournalistic work that you were asked to do when you had been invited for the literature festival there.

'I met X last night. I think he came for my talk, too.'

'That's sweet of him.'

'I told him that you had expressly asked that I should give him your regards.'

'What did he say?'

'He said, "Just tell her to finish the book".'

We laughed.

'Tell him I'm almost done. I'm struggling with the ending. I know how it ends, but I'm still leading up to it. Just another 500 words to go, I think. The thing is, I can't force it. I cannot sit at my desk and command the universe to let the words become flesh. I'll try again today. Maybe it'll happen.'

'Okay.'

'Tell him I may just send it to him today.'

'Don't worry, I'm sure he's too busy to look at it right now.'

My neighbour lured me upstairs soon after our conversation.

'There's lovely sun today. Let's sit on the terrace and have breakfast. I'll make some eggs. You bring the coffee and your French press.'

I couldn't resist her invitation. We lounged in the winter sunlight and spoke of many things. An hour later I managed to stop myself from daydreaming and returned home. I decided to use what I call the Miller technique in the hope that it would help induce labour. This seven-year-old strategy has been my salvation in many such moments when the words refuse to flow through my being. It involves picking up any book by Henry Miller and reading a page at random. Miller's writing is so eternally alive, inspired, and infectious that it incites pathways in my brain and makes my fingers itch for the thrumming of the keyboard. This is the passage I serendipitously chanced upon on page thirty-two of my worn-out copy of *Plexus*:

If I were reading a book and happened to strike a wonderful passage I would close the book then and there and go for a walk. I hated the thought of coming to the end of a good book. I would tease it along, delay the inevitable as long as possible. But always, when I hit a great passage, I would stop reading immediately. Out I would go, rain, hail, snow or ice, and chew the cud. One can become so full with the spirit of another being as to be literally afraid of bursting. Everyone I presume, has had the experience. This 'other being', let me observe, is always a sort of alter ego. *It isn't a mere matter of recognizing a kindred soul, it is a matter of recognizing yourself. To come suddenly face to face with yourself! What a moment! Closing the book you continue the act of creation. And this procedure, this ritual, I should say, is always the same: a communication on all fronts at once. No more barriers. More alone than ever, you are nevertheless glued to the world as never before.* Incorporated in it. *Suddenly it becomes clear to you, that when God made the world He did not abandon it to sit in contemplation—somewhere in limbo. God made the world and He entered into it: that is the meaning of creation.*

Miller ends *Plexus* by foreshadowing the events that will come to pass in *Nexus,* the last book of his autobiographical *Rosy Crucifixion* trilogy.

In the days to come, when it will seem as if I were entombed, when the very firmament threatens to come crashing down upon my head, I shall be forced to abandon everything except what these spirits implanted in me. I shall be crushed, debased, humiliated. I shall be frustrated in every fibre of my being. I shall even take to howling like a dog. But I shall not be utterly lost! Eventually a day is to dawn when, glancing over my life as though it were a story or history, I can detect in it a form, a pattern, a meaning. From then on the word defeat becomes meaningless. It will be impossible ever to relapse.

For on that day I become and I remain one with my creation.

He refers to the act of writing his story as one of opening up a wound. At the heart of his trilogy is the act of suffering, which he knows to be unnecessary, yet crucial. *At the last desperate moment—when once can suffer no more!—something happens which is in the nature of a miracle. The great open wound which was draining the blood of life closes up, the organism blossoms like a rose. One is 'free' at last, and not 'with a yearning for Russia', but with a yearning for ever more freedom, ever more bliss. The tree of life is kept alive not by tears but the knowledge that freedom is real and everlasting.*

While these six years spent with you inscribed under my skin do not constitute suffering, they can, in retrospect, be looked at as a terminal condition. You disrupted my state of being. You awakened in me something more dangerous than hunger, more desperate than fervour, more potent than hatred, and the fit of madness that set in when we first began shows no sign of abating. It is still mid-career. When I began this handbook, I stated in clear ink that I was religiously awaiting the day when it would all be undone, 'when the spell is lifted and I'm no longer consumed by you and you're no longer obsessed with me and we can both return to the way we were before we met—un-entangled, uninhibited by love, committed to no one but ourselves.' But I know now that it is not to be. We continue to be lovers without destination, fated to seek refuge in the transient.

What has changed in the course of this handbook is not the

fact that the world will not allow us the privilege of a future but our knowledge of the freedom we have found in the present.

({})

If the Book of Genesis is to be believed, the first act in the seven-day sequence of creation was the separation of the heavens and the earth. 'Now the earth was formless and empty, darkness was over the surface of the deep, and the Spirit of God was hovering over the waters.' Crucial to the narrative was the issue of illumination without which God couldn't imaginatively proceed. And so He said, 'Let there be light,' and there was light. 'God saw that the light was good, and he separated the light from the darkness. God called the light "day", and the darkness he called "night". And there was evening, and there was morning—the first day.' It was this newborn light that would allow for life.

A few seconds after midnight on the eve of your last birthday, I came to you and wished you. I leaned over the chair upon which you were seated and put my mouth over yours. Your lips parted so that your breath now passed from your being into mine. With your tongue you outlined, ever so slightly, the lining of my lips, all the time enlivening my body with your breath.

We retreated into sleep, our bodies interlocked.

We awoke to sunlight gleaming upon our faces. The quilts that we had tucked over ourselves insulated us from the December chill. I leaned over and kissed you on your mouth.

'I've decided to celebrate your fifty-eighth with fifty-eight kisses,' I announced.

I kissed your eyelids, my fingers traced the light wrinkles on either side. I kissed your forehead, the nape of your neck, your ears, my breath sliding in like whispers. I returned to your lips.

'So will you spread them out during the day?' you asked.

'It'll be hard to keep track,' I said. 'I'd rather indulge you in one go.'

I moved my body so that I was parallel to you. I poised myself so that my knees supported my weight. I pulled the sheet over me to shelter us from the chill. Then I administered to you the forty-eight kisses that were still due, rationing each one across the length of your body, silently engulfing you with my lust, each kiss sufficiently soft, silent, wanting.

After we made love, you rested your face between my breasts. Strong streaks of sunshine invaded the bedroom, illuminating the floor beside the bed.

In that marvellous luminous room laden with the scent of our satiated lust I no longer craved the premise of an ending.

As long as there was this daily promise of light, as long as we continued through our art to chase and archive everything touched by its life-affirming presence, as long as we sustained our pursuit of the act of creation, as long as we persevered in drawing our happiness from the present, our love would retain the purity it had acquired through its disregard for destiny.

'How does it end?'

'It doesn't.'

About the Author

Rosalyn D'Mello is a widely published freelance art writer based in New Delhi and was the editor-in-chief of Blouin Artinfo India. She is a regular contributor to *Vogue, Open, Mint Lounge, Art Review* and *Art Review Asia*. Nominated for Forbes' Best Emerging Art Writer Award in 2014, she was also shortlisted for the inaugural Prudential Eye Art Award for Best Writing on Asian Contemporary Art in 2014. She was associate editor of *The Art Critic*, a selection of the art writings of Richard Bartholomew from the 1950s to the early 1980s and was a member of the jury of the Prudential Eye Art Award 2015.

A Handbook for My Lover is her first book.